I0821998

13 GHOSTS

AWAKENED

13 Ghosts Awakened

This is a work of fiction. Names, characters, places, and incidents are products of the author's imagination or have been used fictitiously and are not to be construed as real. Any resemblance to persons, living or dead, actual events, locales, or organizations is coincidental.

ISBN: 979-8-9907254-0-9 (hardback)
979-8-9893424-9-5 (paperback)

Printed in the United States of America

13 GHOSTS
AWAKENED

GARY J. ROSE

To my beloved family, friends, and fans,

Thank you for standing by me throughout this journey, for your unwavering support and encouragement that keeps inspiring me to continue in my storytelling.

Special gratitude to my dear sister, Debbie Miller, whose keen eye and honest feedback breathed life into the first draft of this tale. Your insight was invaluable, and your belief in me never wavered.

"What I can't accept about spiritualism is the idea of millions of dead people (there must be standing room only on the Other Side) kept hanging about just waiting to be sent for by some old girl with a Ouija board in a Brighton boarding house, or a couple of table-tappers in Tring, for the sake of some inane conversation about the Blueness of the Infinite. I mean at least when you're dead you'll surely be spared such tedious social occasions."

— John Mortimer's barrister in
"Rumpole and the Dear Departed" (1981)

13
COLOR
GHOSTS
ILLUSION-O!

IN HOMAGE

In homage to the original 1960 classic, "*13 Ghosts*," I present a reimagined tale of supernatural intrigue and chilling suspense. The original film was directed and produced by William Castle. He had previously produced *House on Haunted Hill* and *Tingler*, both in 1959. 13 Ghosts, upon release received mixed reviews.

As with several of his more famous productions, producer William Castle used a gimmick to promote *13 Ghosts*, as audience members were given the choice to see the ghosts. In theaters, most scenes were in black-and-white, but scenes involving ghosts were shown in a process dubbed "Illusion-O".

The filmed elements of the actors and the sets–everything except the ghosts–had a blue filter applied to the footage, while the ghost elements had a red filter and were superimposed over the frame. Audiences received viewing glasses with red and blue cellophane filters. Unlike with early 3D glasses having one eye red and the other cyan or blue, the Illusion-O device required viewers to look through a single color with both eyes. Looking through the red filter intensified the images of the ghosts, while the blue filter "removed" them.

Television and home video releases are edited to simulate the effect without the need for special glasses.

Howard Thompson of *The New York Times* called the film "a simple, old-fashioned haunted house yarn" that "would be a lot better off without this gimmick." *Variety* wrote: "The idea is sound and exploitable, but the execution doesn't fully come off," explaining the ghosts "lack personality and aren't frightening, so that there isn't sufficient tension in the sequences during which the 'ghost viewer' comes into play."

The Monthly Film Bulletin called it "a workmanlike but not very frightening horror film... the ghosts, which are a dull red color, are far less effective when witnessed than when their presence is merely suggested, especially when their viewability depends on a process as unremarkable as Illusion-O.

The plot revolved around the occultist Dr. Plato Zorba who bequeaths a large house to his impoverished nephew Cyrus. Along with his wife Hilda, teen daughter Medea and adolescent son, Buck, Cyrus is informed by lawyer Benjamin Rush that the house comes with ghosts that Dr. Zorba has collected from around the world.

The will stipulates that the family must stay in the house and cannot sell it, or it will be turned over to the state. The family is shocked to find that the house is really haunted by 12 ghosts. The furnished mansion also comes with a creepy housekeeper, Elaine, who use to conduct seances, as well as a hidden fortune concealed somewhere on the property.

The spirits include a wailing lady, clutching hands, a fiery skeleton, an Italian chef continuously murdering his wife and her lover in the kitchen, a hanging lady, an executioner holding a severed head, a fully grown lion with its headless tamer, a floating head and a ghost of Zorba himself, all held captive in the eerie house and looking for an unlucky 13th ghost to free them.

Dr. Zorba also leaves a set of special goggles, the only way of seeing the ghosts. A Ouija board warns the family that a death will occur in the house and to the suspense.

Rush, the estate executor, knows Zorba's fortune is hidden somewhere in the house, having unsuccessfully searched for it previously. When two $100 bills fall loose after Buck slides down the stairs, Rush tricks Buck into secretly searching for the money. After Buck finds the cash under the stairs, Rush carries the sleeping boy out of his room and attempts to murder him in the same way that he killed Zorba: using a four-poster bed equipped with a descending canopy that fatally suffocates people.

Zorba's ghost appears, killing Rush by driving the terrified Rush under the canopy as Buck awakens and escapes. Rush has become the 13th ghost. The next morning, Cyrus and his family count the recovered money and decide to stay. Elaine says the ghosts have left but predicts they will return, much to Buck's delight. Unseen by the family, an unseen force blows the special glasses into smithereens. Elaine gets a broom and permits herself a small enigmatic smile.

CHAPTER ONE

IN THE CONFINES of his university office, Professor Donald Sullivan sat ensconced behind his cluttered desk, his brow knitted in profound contemplation. With the weight of his years evident in the slight curve of his posture and the telltale signs of late nights spent in scholarly pursuits, he projected an air of seasoned academia.

His tweed jacket, worn with both scholarly pride and the traces of countless investigations into the realm of debunking the supernatural, draped over a frame that bore the faint evidence of indulgence—a modest beer belly that hinted at a life not entirely consumed by intellectual pursuits.

As he perused the letter resting before him, penned by a Mr. Fred Lawson, Sullivan's lips curled into a faint grimace of disdain. Another charlatan preying upon the vulnerable, he mused silently, casting a discerning gaze upon the image of Madam Zora, the alleged spiritualist, captured in a photograph retrieved from the depths of the Internet.

A firm knock on his office door jolted Sullivan back to the present. With a creak, the door swung open, revealing his graduate students Nancy Taylor, followed closely by Stewart Holden.

"Good morning, Professor," chimed the ever-bubbly Ms. Taylor, her enthusiasm seemingly boundless. Sullivan couldn't help but wonder if her perpetual cheeriness was fueled by something more than just morning coffee; however, upon closer observation, he concluded that it was simply her innate Type-A personality shining through.

Stewart, or Stu as he was often called, sauntered in behind Nancy, his demeanor more relaxed in stark contrast to her vivacity. He seemed to take cues from those around him, embodying a laid-back persona that complemented Nancy's exuberance.

Nancy commanded attention wherever she went. With her long, flowing black hair cascading below her shoulders and piercing green eyes that seemed to hold secrets untold, she possessed a striking allure that captivated those around her. Despite her undeniable beauty, there was an air of mystery about her, an enigmatic quality that hinted at depths beyond her outward appearance.

Unbeknownst to many, Nancy harbored a fierce attraction to the professor, her feelings simmering beneath the surface with an intensity that she struggled to conceal. She found herself drawn to him in ways she couldn't fully explain, her interactions with him often tinged with a subtle undercurrent of flirtation that she couldn't resist indulging in whenever the opportunity arose.

"Another case on our hands?" Nancy leaned in, her gaze fixed on the professor as she rested her arms on his desk, a display of her ample cleavage that bordered on deliberate. "If you were to look up 'fraud' in the dictionary, I'm pretty sure you'd find Madam Zora's picture right there," she remarked with a hint of sarcasm, her tone laced with disdain. "Stu, take a look at her."

Stu leaned in, his gaze focused on the image of Madam Zora. "No doubt about it, she's a con artist," he affirmed. "So, when's the big reveal, Professor? When do we expose her for what she really is?"

Sullivan's lips curved into a fond smile as he regarded his two eager graduate students. Their youthful banter never failed to inject a spark of vitality into his day, reminding him of the boundless curiosity and enthusiasm of youth.

"According to Mr. Lawson's letter, his aunt is set to attend another séance with Zora tonight," Sullivan relayed, his tone tinged with anticipation. "As usual, we'll conduct surveillance outside her establishment, gaining insight into the proceedings. Mr. Lawson will discreetly outfit his aunt with a microphone, allowing us to eavesdrop on Zora's performance within the confines of the séance room. It promises to be quite the spectacle."

Nancy's eyes lit up with anticipation as she interjected, "And then we'll arrange for one of us to go undercover during a session, right?" She couldn't hide her eagerness, already hoping she would be the chosen one for the task ahead.

"Exactly," Sullivan confirmed with a nod. "Stu, ensure the van is fueled up and ready to roll. Double-check our surveillance gear to ensure everything's in working order. Tonight marks the beginning of our investigation into Madam Zora, so no need for recordings just yet. We'll simply observe and listen to the charade unfold."

He glanced at his watch before continuing, "Unfortunately, Mr. Lawson's aunt will likely be out a considerable sum of money, but hopefully, after tonight, we will put an end to that. Be back here by 6:00 PM. It shouldn't take more than 30 minutes to set up near Madam Zora's house. The séance is slated to begin promptly at 7:00 PM." As normal, Nancy was the last to leave.

In a remote, snow-covered corner of Maine, Francis Zorba sat in her car, the engine humming softly as she sought solace in its warmth. Beyond the frosted windshield, a sprawling estate loomed on the hillside, shrouded in a thick blanket of foliage that seemed to swallow the feeble rays of sunlight.

Francis, nearing her fifties, cut a slender figure against the wintry landscape. Her hair, pulled back into a tight bun, betrayed not a single strand out of place, while her choice of eyewear added an air of sophistication that belied her years. Despite her composed exterior, a sense of unease prickled at the edges of her consciousness as she gazed upon the imposing mansion before her.

She picks up a magazine where the corner of a page marked an article. She turned to that page showing a picture of Professor Sullivan being interviewed after his investigation exposed a spiritualist being arrested for fraud. She glanced back at the mansion on the hill and put the magazine down lost in thought.

The Zorba estate, a relic of a bygone era, held a legacy as dark and foreboding as the shadows that enveloped it. As the last descendant of the Zorba clan, Francis bore the weight of her family's history upon her shoulders—a burden she had long sought to escape, yet could never fully evade.

With a shiver that had nothing to do with the biting cold, Francis braced herself for what lay ahead. Little did she know, the secrets that lurked within the walls of the mansion were far more chilling than the winter winds that swept across the mountainside.

CHAPTER TWO

THE VAN, HOUSING Professor Sullivan, Nancy, and Stu, boasted a large side window fitted with a one-way pane of glass, affording those within the vehicle a clear view of the surroundings while preventing prying eyes from peering in.

"Everyone settled in?" Sullivan inquired, casting a quick glance at his watch. "The aunt and nephew should be arriving shortly."

The interior of the van, though compact, had been meticulously arranged to accommodate its occupants comfortably during their surveillance mission. Sullivan's gaze shifted from his watch to the van's rearview mirror, his anticipation increasing as he awaited the arrival of their targets.

Near the window, atop a small table, sat a tape-recording device—an integral component of Professor Sullivan's surveillance setup. Tonight, all three occupants of the van would utilize the pairs of earphones resting beside the device, allowing them to monitor the proceedings within while relying on the audio feed captured by the discreet device attached to Mr. Lawson's unsuspecting aunt.

The glow of headlights pierced the darkness as a car maneuvered into the parking lot, casting its illumination upon a sign adorned with tarot cards and a captivating depiction of Madam Zora. Her piercing, hypnotic gaze seemed to follow the onlooker, captured in a larger-than-life image beside a fortune-teller's crystal ball.

"Let the show begin," an eager Nancy said as she leaned forward towards the side window. The three picked up their earphones and could hear small talk between Mr. Lawson and his aunt. They opened the door to the establishment and walked in. A male's voice could be heard solemly requesting that they enter the parlor where the séance would be held as before.

Sullivan mused that Madam Zora would likely orchestrate a dramatic entrance, adding to the aura of mysticism surrounding the event. As if on cue, the faint sound of her arrival could be discerned, gradually growing louder as she made her way into the room.

"Good evening," Madam Zora's voice rang out, rich with a practiced charm. "I trust the spirits will favor us once more tonight. How are you, Lydia?" she inquired, her words laced with an otherworldly allure.

"Lydia," Sullivan whispered to Nancy and Stu, providing them with the aunt's name. The exchange of pleasantries continued as the group settled in for the evening's proceeding. Suddenly, a small side door creaked open, revealing the figure of the man who had extended the invitation to Mr. Lawson and his aunt, stepping into the parlor.

"Collect intel to provide Madam Zora?" Stu posed the question, his tone tinged with skepticism. It was a rhetorical query, one that underscored the routine nature of their task when investigating fraudulent practitioners like Madam Zora.

As anticipated, the man approached the car with its doors ajar, slipping inside with a casual air. His gaze roamed over the scattered belongings within, seemingly unfazed by their presence. Observing closely, the trio noticed him speaking into what appeared to be a microphone, deducing that his words were likely being transmitted directly to a concealed earpiece worn by Madam Zora.

Sullivan subtly signaled to the group with a thumbs-up, silently acknowledging that the con had commenced and that the information obtained from the search of Lawson's car was now being employed by Madam Zora.

"Mr. Lawson," she began, her voice carrying an otherworldly resonance as she turned her attention to their unwitting subject. "The spirits convey to me that you harbor an interest in sports. Basketball, perhaps? No, not basketball... football, yes?" she ventured, her words laced with a calculated certainty as she delved into the carefully curated details gleaned from the search of Lawson's belongings.

"Yes, how did you know that?" Lawson's surprise was palpable as he responded to Madam Zora's uncanny insight. Sullivan opted not to divulge the inner workings of the fortune teller's techniques, allowing Lawson's astonishment to appear deliberate.

"The spirit world possesses a wisdom that transcends our earthly understanding," Madam Zora replied cryptically, her words imbued with an air of mystique. "But before we can summon them, we must attend to matters of payment, so that I may focus my energies." With a graceful gesture, Lydia passed an envelope bulging with cash to the outstretched hands of Madam Zora, as her nephew looked on distressed.

"Now, we commence," Madam Zora announced solemnly, igniting several candles arranged on the table, their flickering flames casting dancing shadows across the dimly lit room. At the center of the table sat a crystal ball, its surface gleaming faintly in the soft candlelight.

With a deliberate gesture, Madam Zora extinguished the room's overhead lights, enveloping the space in a cloak of darkness pierced only by the wavering glow of the candles. The dim illumination made it challenging to discern the details of the surroundings, adding to the mystique of the moment.

As the room descended into an eerie silence, Madam Zora's demeanor underwent a remarkable transformation. Her movements became fluid, almost ethereal, as if she were channeling energies beyond the realm of mortal comprehension. With eyes closed and hands outstretched over the crystal ball, she began to sway gently, her breaths coming in shallow, rhythmic patterns.

"Alaric... Alaric..." Her voice, barely a whisper, carried an otherworldly resonance as she invoked the name of Mrs. Lawson's long-departed husband. The atmosphere crackled with an inexplicable energy, as if the very air itself hung heavy with the presence of unseen forces.

Suddenly, her body tensed, a tremor coursing through her frame as if a powerful force had taken hold. "Alaric speaks to me," she proclaimed, her voice rising in pitch as she delved deeper into her trance-like state. "He... he has a message for you, Lydia."

With bated breath, the group leaned in, hanging on her every word. It was a well-rehearsed charade, designed to prey upon the vulnerabilities of the unsuspecting. Madam Zora's supposed communication with the spirit realm was a carefully orchestrated performance, utilizing a combination of cold reading, vague statements, and selective memory to create the illusion of supernatural insight.

"Alaric... he wishes to convey his love for you," she intoned, her voice trembling with feigned emotion. "He watches over you still, guiding you from beyond the veil." It was a classic ploy, exploiting the universal desire for connection with departed loved ones to elicit a sense of comfort and validation.

Meanwhile, unseen to the unsuspecting onlookers, Sullivan and his team monitored the proceedings closely, their ears attuned to every word uttered by Madam Zora. The microphone discreetly affixed to Mr. Lawson's aunt provided a direct feed of the conversation, allowing them to intercept and analyze the fraudulent claims being made.

As Madam Zora continued her performance, weaving a tapestry of lies and half-truths, Sullivan made mental notes of each manipulation and deception employed. It was a familiar dance, one he had witnessed countless times before in his quest to expose the charlatans who preyed upon the vulnerable and the gullible.

And so, the charade unfolded, each carefully crafted illusion serving to deepen the web of deceit spun by Madam Zora and her ilk. But behind the veil of mysticism and manipulation, Sullivan and his team remained vigilant, poised to expose the truth and bring an end to the reign of fraudulent fortune tellers once and for all.

"I think we've heard enough. Let's head back to the university. I will call Mr. Lawson later this evening and let him know we will take the case."

CHAPTER THREE

"PROFESSOR, YOUR CLASS is waiting for you in lecture hall one," Stu announced, breezing into Sullivan's office without so much as a knock. His tone carried a hint of urgency, indicating the imminent commencement of the lecture. "Looks like a full house," he remarked, glancing over his shoulder.

Sullivan arched an eyebrow, his expression betraying mild surprise at the news. "Introduction to Parapsychology usually is," he remarked wryly, closing the textbook he had been perusing and reaching for his briefcase. With a practiced motion, he slung it over his shoulder, ready to embark on his next academic endeavor.

As they made their way to lecture hall one, Sullivan couldn't help but notice the buzz of excitement permeating the corridors. The sound of eager chatter spilled forth from the open doorway, mingling with the shuffling of feet and the occasional burst of laughter. Always present during the first day of a new semester, he thought.

Upon entering the lecture hall, Sullivan's gaze swept over the sea of eager faces, noting with satisfaction the overflow of students that filled every available seat and spilled into the aisles. It was a testament to the enduring fascination with the paranormal, a subject that never failed to captivate the imagination of both believers and skeptics alike.

With a nod of acknowledgment, Sullivan made his way to the lectern, his presence commanding the attention of the room. "Good morning, everyone," he greeted, his voice projecting effortlessly over the hum of conversation. "It's wonderful to see such a turnout for our first class of the semester."

As he began his lecture, Sullivan couldn't help but feel a sense of satisfaction at the prospect of sharing his knowledge with such a receptive audience. He knew from experience that while the initial enthusiasm might wane for some, there would always be a core group of students eager to delve deeper into the mysteries of the unknown.

And so, as the lecture unfolded, Sullivan guided his students on a journey through the realms of parapsychology, exploring the intricacies of psychic phenomena, ghostly encounters, and the mysteries of the human mind. With each passing moment, the lines between skepticism and belief blurred, replaced by a shared curiosity and thirst for knowledge.

By the end of the class, Sullivan was pleased to see that the spark of curiosity had been ignited in many of his students, their minds abuzz with questions and theories. As they filed out of the lecture hall, he couldn't help but feel a sense of optimism for the semester ahead, knowing that he had the opportunity to shape the minds of the next generation of paranormal investigators and truth-seekers.

His meticulously curated syllabus was no stranger to the art of academic attrition. With a judicious selection of readings and assignments, Professor Sullivan anticipated that at least 5% of his enrollment would likely succumb to the rigors of the course, their ranks thinned by the weight of scholarly expectations.

Yet, it wasn't just the scholarly hurdles that would weed out the faint-hearted. Another 2% of the initial hopefuls, drawn by the allure of a seemingly easy credit, would inevitably vanish into the ether once faced with the reality of a challenging curriculum. Those who had sauntered into the lecture hall on the first day, hoping for a leisurely stroll through the subject matter, would soon find themselves confronted with the daunting task of absorbing nearly seventy-five pages of dense text and supplementary materials in preparation for Sullivan's inaugural lecture.

But for now, Sullivan's focus was elsewhere. While his mind buzzed with academic anticipation, a more immediate concern tugged at his thoughts: the scheduled séance between Madam Zora and his intrepid students, Nancy and Stu, slated for this very evening.

As he reviewed his notes and double-checked the logistics of the surveillance operation, Sullivan couldn't shake the sense of excitement that tingled in the air. The prospect of exposing Madam Zora's charade held a certain allure, a tantalizing blend of academic pursuit and investigative intrigue that fueled his passion for unraveling the mysteries of the paranormal.

With a determined nod, Sullivan set aside his academic duties for the moment, fully immersing himself in the preparations for the evening's clandestine operation. The fate of the course enrollment could wait; tonight, the truth would be revealed, and the forces of deception would be laid bare before the discerning eyes of reason and skepticism.

Perched atop the hill like a silent sentinel, the Zorba estate cast a shadow over the surrounding landscape, its weathered facade bearing witness to decades of abandonment and neglect. For over sixty years, its once-grand halls had echoed only with the whispers of memories long forgotten, its rooms shrouded in the dusty cloak of solitude.

Only one figure dared to defy the desolate silence that gripped the estate: Elaine, the enigmatic recluse known to the locals as the 'witch' of Zorba Manor. The nickname given to her by Buck, the youngest member of the Zorba family of four, and the other curious souls who dared to venture near, she was a figure of mystery and intrigue, her presence casting a spell of unease over the decaying mansion.

The turning point came with the discovery of hidden treasure nestled within the ancient staircase of the mansion—a cache of long-forgotten riches that had lain dormant for generations. The money had been stashed away from the spiritislist and elder Zorba for unknown reasons. With the revelation of this hidden bounty, the Zorba family hastily fled the estate, their departure shrouded in secrecy and haste. Yet, amidst the rush to escape, Elaine remained, a solitary figure haunting the halls of the abandoned mansion like a ghost of the past.

As the years wore on, Elaine's presence became increasingly elusive, her once-bold footsteps fading into the echoes of memory. Eventually, she too succumbed to the inexorable march of time, her final days spent in a haze of confusion and delirium, wandering the hillside with whispered words that none could decipher.

In the end, Elaine passed away peacefully in her sleep, her enigmatic secrets buried with her in the cold earth. With her passing, the Zorba estate reverted back to the state, a silent monument to a bygone era of opulence and intrigue.

Yet, despite the state's best efforts to entice potential buyers, the mansion remained a forsaken relic of the past, its halls overrun by spiders, roaches, and rats. And yet, amidst the decay and neglect, a curious phenomenon persisted: Mother Nature herself seemed to refuse to reclaim the land upon which the estate stood.

Was it simply the relentless march of time that held the mansion in its icy grip, or was there something more sinister at play? Whispers of ghostly apparitions and otherworldly presences lingered in the air, lending an eerie pallor to the desolate landscape. Whatever the truth may be, the Zorba estate stood as a testament to the mysteries of the past, a silent witness to the secrets that lay buried beneath its crumbling facade.

CHAPTER FOUR

NANCY AND STU had meticulously memorized the script handed to them by Professor Sullivan, their lines etched into their minds through countless rehearsals. What had once been a thrilling challenge had now become a monotonous routine, the thrill of anticipation dulled by familiarity. Still, they understood the importance of their roles in Professor Sullivan's elaborate scheme to expose Madam Zora's deceit, and they were prepared to play their parts to perfection.

Nancy, with her flair for drama and an unwavering belief in the occult, was poised to take center stage as the grieving sister of Danny, her beloved older brother tragically taken from her in a motorcycle accident in Los Angeles. Her fervent belief in the supernatural often clashed with the skepticism of her younger brother, Stewart, whose pragmatic nature served as a counterbalance to Nancy's unwavering faith in the unseen.

When the male attendant at Madam Zora's establishment answered the phone, Nancy spun a tale of grief and desperation with practiced ease. Her words, laden with sorrow and urgency, seemed to strike a chord with the man on the other end of the line, who readily swallowed the fabricated storyline. Nancy even went so far as to mention a sizable inheritance from her deceased brother, insinuating that she was willing to pay handsomely for a séance conducted on short notice.

The séance was swiftly arranged for 7 pm the following night, now looming on the horizon like a gathering storm. As the evening drew near, Nancy and Stu couldn't help but feel a flutter of anticipation mingled with apprehension. The stage was set, the players in position, and the game of cat and mouse with Madam Zora was about to begin in earnest.

Nancy discreetly concealed a hidden wire beneath her bra, its thin, wiry form snaking its way beneath the fabric of her sheer black sweater. Meanwhile, Stu donned a pair of glasses outfitted with tiny lenses discreetly attached near the glass lenses, poised to transmit a live feed of his perspective during the impending charade. With Sullivan stationed in the university van, would be ready to record and monitor the proceedings remotely, the trio was primed for their undercover operation.

As they embarked on their journey to Madam Zora's residence, Stu assumed the role of chauffeur, his expression betraying a mix of skepticism and resignation. Nancy, the grieving sister of the deceased and a staunch believer in the supernatural, sat beside him, her nerves coiled tightly beneath a facade of determined resolve.

Strategically scattered across the rear seat of the vehicle were magazines detailing the latest advancements in civilian drones, a deliberate ploy to maintain the illusion of an innocent outing. Each magazine had been meticulously photographed prior to their departure from the university, showing their position in the vehicle they hoped Madam Zora's accomplish would find during his search of the car.

A block away from their destination, Stu brought the car to a halt, allowing Sullivan to proceed ahead and covertly park the van across the street from Madam Zora's residence. With their surveillance post established, the trio resumed their journey.

As they pulled into the parking lot of Madam Zora's establishment, a sense of tension settled over them like a suffocating blanket. With each passing moment, the stakes grew higher, the uncertainty of what lay ahead looming ominously on the horizon. But with their preparations complete and their resolve unshakeable, Nancy and Stu approached the entrance of Madam Zora.

As they rapped upon the door, it swung open to reveal a tall, somber figure cloaked in black, his demeanor lending an air of solemnity to the dimly lit hallway. To Nancy, he seemed a perfect candidate for a Halloween costume contest, his attire reminiscent of a mortician preparing for the final rites. With a polite nod, Nancy introduced herself and Stu but received only a slight smile from their greeter.

With a gesture of acknowledgment, the solemn figure ushered them into the dimly lit séance room, its walls adorned with ornate Victorian decorations that seemed to exude an aura of antiquated mystique. Stu's glasses, ever vigilant, captured the scene with meticulous precision, their tiny lenses transmitting the image of a room steeped in shadow and mystery.

As they settled into their seats, the greeter departed with a nod, leaving Nancy and Stu alone in the dimly lit room, their senses heightened by the anticipation of what was to come. The air crackled with an indefinable energy, a sense of expectancy hanging heavy in the atmosphere like a shroud.

With each passing moment, the silence deepened, broken only by the faint whisper of the wind outside and the rhythmic ticking of an antique clock. Time seemed to stretch and warp in the dimly lit room, the minutes dragging by like hours as they waited for the arrival of Madam Zora. Both surmised that their car was probably being searched.

And then, like a specter emerging from the shadows, she appeared—a vision in flowing robes and mysterious allure, her presence commanding the attention of all who beheld her. With a regal grace, she swept into the room, her gaze penetrating and enigmatic as she took her place at the head of the table.

"I am Madam Zora," she declared, her words tinged with what seemed to be a contrived Romanian accent. "You are Nancy, and you, the skeptic younger brother, Stewart." Her gaze fixed on Stu, a knowing glint dancing in her eyes. "And Stewart, the spirits are speaking to me. They advise against purchasing the model you have in mind. No, wait. It's not a model. It's a drone." She paused dramatically, drawing out the suspense. "You're considering a drone, aren't you? Yes, the spirits are adamant that you should conduct more research before making any hasty decisions."

The revelation sent a chill down Nancy's spine, confirming their suspicions that their cover had not been compromised. It was hard for the two to suppress laughter as the fraud was playing out. The greeter's seemingly innocuous demeanor now revealed itself as a calculated ploy to gather information about them, casting a shadow of doubt over their entire operation. Stu, playing his part to perfection, feigned disbelief at Madam Zora's uncanny insight, his expression a mask of incredulity.

As the tension in the room reached its zenith, Nancy and Stu braced themselves for the impending séance, their hearts pounding with a mixture of anticipation and apprehension. With each passing moment, the line between reality and illusion blurred, their resolve tested by the enigmatic forces that surrounded them.

With a sense of trepidation, they prepared to delve into the mysteries of the spirit world, their determination unwavering in the face of whatever truths or deceptions awaited them. The séance was about to begin, and Nancy and Stu stood ready to confront the unknown, their fate hanging in the balance as they embarked on a journey into the depths of the supernatural.

As the séance commenced, Madam Zora's attempts to make contact with the spirit of Danny, Nancy and Stu's deceased brother, seemed to falter. Despite her best efforts to bridge the gap between the living and the dead, the room remained shrouded in an eerie silence, broken only by the faint whisper of the wind outside.

With furrowed brow and a sense of frustration mounting, Madam Zora pressed on, her voice taking on a note of urgency as she implored the spirits to make their presence known. But the crystal ball before her remained ominously still, its surface unyielding to her entreaties.

As minutes stretched into hours, the tension in the room grew palpable, a sense of unease settling over Nancy and Stu like a suffocating fog. The air seemed to thicken with anticipation, the atmosphere crackling with the latent energy of the unknown.

And then, just when all hope seemed lost, a subtle shift occurred—a faint tremor rippling through the room as if an unseen force had been awakened from its slumber. The crystal ball, once inert and lifeless, began to shimmer with an ethereal glow, its surface swirling with wisps of ghostly smoke.

A low, mournful wail echoed through the room, sending shivers down Nancy and Stu's spines as they exchanged wary glances. It was as if the very fabric of reality was unraveling before their eyes, the boundary between the living and the dead growing ever more porous with each passing moment.

And then, in a crescendo of supernatural power, the table beneath them began to lift, its legs trembling under the weight of an unseen force. Nancy and Stu watched in awe as the room filled with an otherworldly light, casting long shadows that danced across the walls like spectral apparitions.

With a triumphant cry, Madam Zora announced that she had made contact with Danny's spirit, her voice ringing out with a mixture of awe and reverence. The séance had reached its climax, the veil between the realms of the living and the dead torn asunder as the spirit of Danny made his presence known in a dazzling display of spectral power.

In a voice tinged with a deep, faux Romanian accent, Madam Zora assumed the persona of the departed Danny, her words carrying an otherworldly resonance as she addressed Nancy and Stu. With a solemn nod, she welcomed them to the séance, her eyes shining with an unearthly light as she conveyed Danny's message from beyond the grave.

"My dear sister and brother," she intoned, her voice echoing with a spectral timbre. "I greet you with love and longing from the realm beyond. Know that I am at peace, free from the burdens of earthly suffering. Though my time here is fleeting, I want you to know that I am surrounded by love and light."

As Nancy and Stu listened, their hearts heavy with grief yet buoyed by the hope of connection, Madam Zora continued to channel Danny's spirit, his words a balm to their wounded souls. "I miss you both more than words can express," he murmured, his voice suffused with a bittersweet longing. "But fear not, for our bond transcends the boundaries of life and death."

With each passing moment, the veil between the worlds grew thinner, allowing Danny's spirit to reach out to his beloved siblings with words of comfort and reassurance. "There is much I wish to share with you," he confessed, his voice tinged with regret. "But the mysteries of the afterlife are vast, and my time here is limited. We will need to convene several more times before I can fully reveal the depths of my soul."

And so, the séance drew to a close, leaving Nancy and Stu with a sense of both awe and anticipation. Though their hearts ached with the absence of their beloved brother, they found solace in the knowledge that his spirit remained with them, guiding and protecting them from beyond the veil. And as they prepared to depart, the male greeter arranged for their next séance in two days.

Within the confines of the van, every moment of the séance had been meticulously captured on video. As Nancy and Stu departed the parking lot, Sullivan remained behind for a few minutes, ensuring their safe departure before embarking on the journey back to the university. The evidence they had gathered of Madam Zora's fraudulent activities would soon be in the hands of a special prosecutor, a trusted ally who had collaborated on numerous successful investigations with Professor Sullivan.

With a sense of satisfaction, Sullivan envisioned the downfall of Madam Zora's deceitful enterprise. He knew that when Mr. Lawson's aunt attended their next séance under the watchful eye of their operation by law enforcement, the truth would be revealed, and the charade would be brought to an abrupt end. The wheels of justice were set in motion, and Madam Zora's days of preying upon the vulnerable were numbered.

CHAPTER FIVE

AS THE DUST settled on his latest successful expose of fraudulent spiritual practices, Professor Sullivan found himself back in the familiar confines of his cluttered office, surrounded by the remnants of countless investigations. The faint scent of old books mingled with the crisp air of determination that permeated the room, a testament to the relentless pursuit of truth that defined his career.

As he settled into his worn leather chair, Sullivan's thoughts turned to their next steps. Little did he know, an unexpected visitor was about to disrupt the calm of his sanctuary, setting into motion a chain of events that would test his resolve like never before.

Meanwhile, in a remote corner of Maine, Francis Zorba sat alone in her hotel room, her mind consumed by thoughts of the past and the weight of her family's legacy. Haunted by the secrets that lay buried within its walls of the Zorba estate, Francis felt the pull of destiny drawing her inexorably towards the one man who could help her uncover the truth.

With a sense of determination born of desperation, she resolved to seek out Professor Sullivan, knowing that their meeting would mark the beginning of a journey fraught with peril and possibility. And so, as the sun dipped below the horizon and the shadows lengthened across the land, Francis Zorba set out on her fateful journey, her path destined to intersect with that of Professor Sullivan in ways neither could have foreseen.

"In our inaugural lecture on Parapsychology and the occult, let's begin with a simple inquiry," Professor Sullivan addressed his class, the lecture hall once again teeming with eager students. "A show of hands, please. How many of you believe in ghosts?"

As hands shot up across the room, Sullivan surveyed the sea of faces before him, noting the overwhelming majority who held firm to their belief in the supernatural. "I see over 80% of you believe in ghosts," he remarked, a note of intrigue coloring his tone. "Now, for my next question. How many of you have actually seen a ghost?"

As more hands rose into the air, Sullivan couldn't help but feel a sense of anticipation building within the room. Despite the skepticism that often pervaded academia, it was clear that the allure of the unknown held a powerful sway over his students. "Still, well over half of the class," he observed, a faint smile playing at the corners of his lips.

"Spiritualism, the notion that the deceased maintain a line of communication with the living, surged in popularity across America and Europe during the 1850s. This movement captivated many Victorians, especially those who were beginning to drift away from traditional religious beliefs. Despite the Victorian era's reputation for scientific and technological advancement, a significant portion of society harbored a deep fascination with the paranormal, supernatural, and occult."

"In the late Victorian period, numerous phenomena gained traction, including mesmerism, clairvoyance, electro-biology, crystal-gazing, and thought-reading. However, Spiritualism emerged as the foremost preoccupation among these pursuits. Figures like Sir Arthur Conan Doyle epitomized this fascination, drawn to the tantalizing prospect of communicating with departed souls."

"Even amidst an age of enlightenment and progress, the allure of the unknown held a powerful sway over the hearts and minds of many Victorians, leaving an indelible mark on the cultural landscape of the era."

"It is generally agreed that the modern Spiritualist movement began on April 1, 1848, in the village of Hydesville, New York, when two teenaged sisters, Margaret and Kate Fox, claimed that they had communicated with the ghost of a man murdered at the house years before their family moved in."

"Reports of this event first appeared in the *New York Tribune* and subsequently in other newspapers in America and Europe. The core belief of Spiritualism was that the living could communicate with the dead through the help of a medium endowed with a supernatural gift during mysterious and entertaining séance phenomena. Within the late Victorian counterculture of Spiritualism, a number of women and men gained renown and authority as skilled mediums."

"Modern Spiritualism, a 'strange and fascinating American import', emerged in Britain in 1852, when the American Maria B. Hayden (1826-1883) visited London and offered her services as a medium. She conducted séances of table rappings and spirit messages for a guinea per head (five guineas for ten). In short time similar séances were offered by a host of local mediums."

"During the late Victorian era, a significant portion of society reported experiencing communication with spirits. This phenomenon, known as Victorian Spiritualism or the Spiritualism movement, gained prominence in the late nineteenth century and drew individuals from various social strata, including Queen Victoria herself. Notably, Victorian Spiritualism held particular appeal for women, who were often perceived as possessing greater spiritual sensitivity than men."

"Female mediums, in particular, were highly regarded within the Spiritualism community, believed to possess a natural aptitude for facilitating communication with the spiritual realm. This preference stemmed from the notion that women had an inherent predisposition toward spiritual perfection. Interestingly, Spiritualism intersected with the broader discourse surrounding women's rights during this period."

"Spiritualists advocated for the recognition of women's rights, addressing what was commonly referred to as the "Woman Question." In doing so, they sought to challenge traditional gender roles and promote gender equality within society. This alignment between Spiritualism and feminist ideals underscored the movement's progressive and socially transformative aspirations during the late Victorian era."

"And it is no accident that Spiritualism, a movement which privileged women and took them seriously, attracted so many female believers during a period of gender disjunction and disparity between aspiration and reality. Spiritualist culture held possibilities for attention, opportunity, and status denied elsewhere. In certain circumstances, it could also provide a means of circumventing rigid nineteenth-century class and gender norms. More importantly, it did so without mounting a direct attack on the status quo. Spiritualism had the potential, not always consciously realized, for subversion."

As Sullivan's lecture dragged on, he was delighted to see that most of his students, the ones not playing video games on their cellphones, were very engaged. He concluded his lecture by letting his students know where their vote about 'do you believe in ghosts' fell in with the general population.

"According to a 2021 YouGov study, 41% of Americans profess a belief in ghosts. Another 20% of those surveyed expressed uncertainty regarding their belief in the supernatural phenomenon. Interestingly, a slightly larger proportion, 43% of Americans polled, believe in the existence of demons."

"For next week's lectures you should have read chapters 12-16. We will review Hollywood's cravings for anything occult. Haunted houses, demon possession, and the various forms of communicating with the dead. Hope you all have a safe weekend."

"Oh. One more thing. For all the Ghostbuster enthusiasts out there, let's address the idea of cameras capturing images of ghosts or spirit beings. While this notion is popular in the paranormal community, it lacks scientific evidence to support it. Claims of such images are often met with skepticism and could be attributed to camera glitches, pareidolia (the tendency to perceive meaningful images in random stimuli), or hoaxes. Scientific consensus stands firm that there's no credible evidence for cameras capturing images of ghosts or spirits.

As there's no scientific basis for the existence of ghosts, there's no "best" camera for seeing something unproven. While infrared, heat, and cold sensors are used to detect temperature changes, they're not designed for capturing images of supernatural entities. If photography interests you, I can offer information on cameras for various purposes or tips for different types of images.

"But, if you wish to make your own "scientific investigation, be my guest but remember; when investigating ghost sightings, it's crucial to approach it scientifically. (A slide is projected on a large screen behind him.) Though ghosts lack scientific backing, scientific methods can explore alternative explanations:

1. **Critical Observation and Documentation:** Encourage detailed, objective accounts of experiences, noting date, time, location, and specifics. Look for patterns among different accounts.
2. **Environmental Analysis:** Examine the physical environment, considering factors like electromagnetic fields, temperature fluctuations, or infrasound that may influence perceptions.
3. **Controlled Experiments:** Conduct experiments to test specific claims, attempting to recreate conditions and observe any natural explanations.
4. **Data Collection:** Use scientific instruments to record relevant data during sightings, such as temperature, humidity, or electromagnetic fields, and analyze for correlations.

5. **Psychological Factors:** Consider psychological aspects like suggestibility and belief systems, as they influence perception.
6. **Collaboration with Experts:** Collaborate with experts from psychology, neuroscience, or physics to gain insights and alternative explanations.

Remember, investigating paranormal claims aims to identify natural explanations, not confirm ghosts' existence. Approach with skepticism and adhere to scientific principles. Have a great rest of the day."

As Professor Sullivan sits in his office, the day's events swirling through his mind, a sudden knock interrupts his thoughts. Startled, he glances toward the door, wondering who could be visiting him at this hour.

"Come in," he calls, straightening in his chair. The door creaks open, revealing a figure silhouetted against the dimly lit hallway. A hunched form with gray hair steps tentatively into the room.

"Excuse me, Professor," the figure says, her voice trembling slightly. "I hope I'm not intruding."

"Not at all," the professor replies, gesturing for the visitor to take a seat. "Please, have a seat. How can I help you?" The figure settles into the chair opposite him, their features obscured by the shadows. Professor Sullivan guesses at her age to be in the seventies. Her gray hair pulled tightly in a bun while wearing a pair of wire framed glasses.

"I couldn't help but overhear your lecture earlier," she begins, her voice raspy with age. "Your theories on the supernatural were quite intriguing." Sullivan offers a polite nod, though he can't help but wonder what this unexpected visitor wants from him.

"Thank you," he replies cautiously. "But forgive me for asking, what brings you here?" The figure hesitates for a moment before speaking again, her voice barely above a whisper.

"You see, Professor," she said slowly, "I come from a family with a... long history of belief in the paranormal. And I couldn't help but wonder if you might be able to help me with a... matter of great importance."

The professor's interest is piqued despite himself. "Go on," he urges, his curiosity now fully aroused. The figure takes a deep breath, as if gathering their thoughts.

"I fear that something... sinister might soon be unleashed upon the world," she continued, her voice filled with dread. "Something that only someone with your expertise can understand."

The hairs on the back of the professor's neck stand on end as he listens to the figure's words. He may not fully believe in the supernatural, but there's no denying the urgency in her voice.

"I'm listening," he says, his curiosity now fully ignited. "Let's start at the beginning. Can I ask you for your name?"

CHAPTER SIX

"My name is Francis Zorba," she begins, her voice carrying a weight of both lineage and mystery. She waits, a fraction of a second, as if expecting her surname to trigger some recognition in Professor Sullivan. It doesn't, but she presses on nonetheless. "My great uncle was Dr. Plato Zorba. He was an occultist who spent his life collecting ghosts. This was over sixty-years ago."

Professor Sullivan's eyebrows raise imperceptibly at the mention of ghosts, his skepticism evident in the subtle tightening of his jaw. Despite his disbelief in the occult, he maintains a courteous demeanor, intrigued by the woman's persistence.

"Dr. Plato Zorba," he repeats, the name sounding foreign on his tongue. "I can't say I'm familiar with his work."

Francis Zorba nods, seemingly unfazed by his lack of recognition. "He was... unconventional, to say the least," she continues, her eyes distant as if recalling memories long buried. "But his research was groundbreaking. He believed that spirits could be captured and contained, cataloged like specimens in a museum."

The professor leans back in his chair, his interest piqued despite himself. "And what does this have to do with your visit to my office?" he asks, his tone carefully neutral.

Francis Zorba's gaze sharpens, as if assessing the professor's reaction. "I've come to you, Professor Sullivan, because I believe that something my great uncle unleashed has resurfaced," she explains, her voice tinged with urgency. "And I fear that it poses a threat to us all."

Despite his skepticism, Professor Sullivan can't help but feel a twinge of unease at the intensity of her words. He may not believe in ghosts, but there's no denying the sincerity in Francis Zorba's eyes.

"I see," he says slowly, his mind racing with questions. "Perhaps you should start at the beginning."

"Dr. Zorba dedicated his life to the study of the supernatural. He traveled the world, seeking out haunted locations and collecting the restless spirits that dwelled within them. He believed that by studying these entities, he could unlock the secrets of the afterlife."

Professor Sullivan listens intently, despite his reservations. There's something captivating about Francis Zorba's tale, something that ignites a spark of curiosity within him.

"He documented his findings in a series of journals," Francis continues, her eyes glittering with a mixture of reverence and fear. She reaches into a large purse and pulls out the journals placing them on Sullivan's desk.

"I think, after you read my great uncles journals, you will understand how he collected his ghosts and the stories behind each one of them. By the time of his death, he became ghost number twelve. The thirteenth ghost was added later. It is another story. Each of the thirteenth ghosts became more powerful and malevolent than the last."

The professor's skepticism wavers for a moment as he considers her words. Could there be some truth to this tale of spectral entities and ancient mysteries?

"And what happened to these thirteen ghosts?" he asks, unable to conceal the curiosity in his voice.

Francis Zorba's expression darkens, a shiver running down her spine. "That, Professor Sullivan," she says gravely, "is what I've come to discuss."

Just as the weight of her words settles over the room, there's a sudden knock on the professor's door, breaking the tension. In strides Nancy and Stu, unaware of the solemn atmosphere.

"Oh, sorry Professor. We didn't know you had a guest. We will come back later," Nancy says, her embarrassment only slight.

"No, that is alright. Please come in, you two," Professor Sullivan says warmly. "You will love the story you are about to hear. Ms. Zorba, these are my two graduate students, Nancy and Stewart."

Zorba remains silent, her gaze fixed on Professor Sullivan. He, in turn, turns to her with a question in his eyes. "Is that okay with you, Ms. Zorba?" he asks.

"Fine," she replies curtly, waiting for the two students to take a seat before continuing. "For years, my great uncle traveled all parts of the world researching legends and rumors of ghosts that inhabited the living. He perfected a method of trapping them and then placed them in his estate."

"Wow! You mean an estate haunted by not one, but many spirits," Nancy interjects excitedly, her curiosity piqued, only to be interrupted by a sharp look from Francis, halting her mid-sentence.

As Sullivan reached for one of the journals of Dr. Plato Zorba, Francis placed her stern hand on it, closing it firmly. "Please, Professor. Let me complete my story," she said, her tone commanding.

Sullivan, caught off guard, quickly withdrew his hand, offering an apologetic nod. He redirected his attention back to Francis, ready to hear what she had to say next.

Francis Zorba's gaze held a haunted intensity as she began to weave the tale of the original plot of 13 ghosts.

"My great uncle, Dr. Plato Zorba, was an enigmatic figure," she began, her voice tinged with reverence and unease. "Over sixty years ago, he delved into the depths of the occult, driven by an insatiable curiosity about the supernatural."

"He dedicated his life to the pursuit of understanding ghosts and spirits," she continued, her words carrying the weight of decades-old memories. "Dr. Zorba traveled the world, scouring ancient texts and folklore for clues to the mysteries of the afterlife."

"He believed that these entities could be captured, contained, and studied," Francis explained, her voice growing somber. "And so, he devised a method to trap them, imprisoning them within the walls of his sprawling estate."

"There, in the dark recesses of his mansion, he amassed a collection of thirteen ghosts," she revealed, her words hanging heavy in the air. "Each one more powerful and malevolent than the last, their tortured souls trapped for eternity."

Francis paused, as if the weight of her words bore down upon her. "But the true horror of Dr. Zorba's experiments was yet to be revealed," she whispered, her voice barely above a whisper.

As she recounted the tale, the room seemed to grow colder, the shadows lengthening ominously around them. And in that moment, Professor Sullivan couldn't shake the feeling that they were on the precipice of something truly terrifying.

"After his passing, the mansion fell into the hands of the state," Francis Zorba recounted, her voice tinged with sorrow. "It remained empty, save for one soul—

Elaine, the housekeeper. But Elaine was more than just a caretaker. She dabbled in the occult, conducting séances within the walls of the estate."

"As for my great uncle, in a twist of fate, he made a decision that would shroud his legacy in mystery," Francis continued, her words heavy with significance. "He withdrew his fortunes from banks and liquidated stocks and bonds, hiding away the wealth somewhere on the property. Only his attorney, Benjamin Rush, was privy to this clandestine transaction—a decision that would seal his fate as the thirteenth ghost."

Stu, unable to contain his curiosity, interjected with a question. "Excuse me, Ms. Zorba. We came in late. Do you mean to say that there are 13 ghosts right now in this estate?"

Francis Zorba's gaze turned somber, her eyes betraying a hint of fear. "Yes," she replied, her voice barely above a whisper. "Thirteen restless souls, trapped within the confines of that mansion, each one harboring secrets and sorrows beyond comprehension."

Silence enveloped the room until Sullivan broke it. "What do you know about these 13 ghosts you reference?"

Francis could sense skepticism in Sullivan's question. "Professor, from your lecture today, and your reputation of exposing spiritualists as fraud agents leading to their day with justice, I know deep in your heart, you have already discounted the validity of what I have revealed. Nonetheless, I will answer your question."

"The spirits include a wailing lady, clutching hands, a fiery skeleton, an Italian chef continuously murdering his wife and her lover in the kitchen, an executioner holding a severed head, a fully grown lion with its headless tamer, a floating head and a ghost of Zorba himself, all held captive in the eerie house and the addition of unlucky 13, Benjamin Rush."

"After the state discovered a descendant of Dr. Zorba, a nephew named Cyrus Zorba, along with his family—his wife Hilda, their older daughter Medea, and young son Buck—their lives became intertwined with the dark legacy of the estate. Benjamin Rush, the executor of the estate, knew of Zorba's hidden fortune, having previously searched for it in vain."

"When two $100 bills unexpectedly fall from a hidden stash after Buck's playful slide down the stairs, Rush seizes the opportunity to manipulate the situation. He convinces Buck to secretly hunt for more money within the house. However, Rush's true intentions are far more sinister."

"After Buck uncovers the hidden cash beneath the stairs, Rush carries the sleeping boy to a four-poster bed, intending to replicate Dr. Zorba's demise by suffocating him with the descending canopy—a macabre echo of the past."

"But as Rush enacts his nefarious plan, Dr. Zorba's ghost materializes, exacting swift and vengeful justice.

The terrified Rush meets his end under the same canopy intended for Buck, becoming the thirteenth ghost."

"The following morning, Cyrus and his family count the recovered money and decide to leave the house, oblivious to the horrors that transpired the night before. Elaine, the housekeeper, assures them that the ghosts have departed, though she ominously predicts their inevitable return."

"These ghosts. How could your great uncle keep track of them?" Sullivan inquired, his skepticism evident in his furrowed brow. Before responding, Francis once again delved into her oversized purse, retrieving a wooden box which she placed beside the journals.

"These glasses," she explained, gesturing towards the box, "allow a person to perceive the presence of the ghosts. After capturing a spirit, my great uncle designated specific locations within the mansion for their containment. For instance, the chef and his wife are confined to the kitchen, while the lion and lion master reside in the basement, and so forth."

"How did he manage to contain them?" Nancy interjected eagerly, beating Stu to the question.

"Each room or area is adorned with sacred inscriptions at all entry and exit points," Francis elaborated, her voice tinged with a hint of solemnity. "These writings act as barriers, delineating the boundaries within which the spirits are confined.

Somehow, the ghosts inherently recognize and respect these boundaries."

As the weight of her words settled over the room, Francis fell silent, the gravity of the situation hanging heavy in the air.

CHAPTER SEVEN

"NOW THAT YOU'VE shared this history," Professor Sullivan began, his curiosity piqued, "what brings you to me?"

Francis paused, her gaze steady as she considered her response. "In the past," she began slowly, "the ghosts seemed to be bound by a tragic cycle, replaying events that tethered them to this world. But everything changed when Benjamin Rush became the thirteenth ghost."

Her words floated in the air like a spirit, the weight of their implications settling over the room.

"Rush was responsible for the murder of my great uncle," Francis continued, her voice trembling with suppressed emotion, "and the attempted murder of Buck, the young boy who found the hidden money in the staircase. His presence in the mansion has ignited a thirst for vengeance among the other twelve spirits."

As she spoke, a chill seemed to creep into the room, the shadows lengthening ominously around them. Professor Sullivan couldn't help but feel a sense of foreboding at the revelation.

"Now," Francis concluded, her voice barely above a whisper, "the ghosts are no longer content to simply replay their past tragedies. They hunger for blood, and unless we intervene, I fear that the consequences will be catastrophic."

"And the estate now? Where is it located?" Stu's voice cut through the tension, breaking the eerie stillness that had settled over the room.

"It's in upper state Maine. That's where a passerby found me several weeks ago," Francis replied, her tone tinged with a hint of unease.

"I don't understand," Professor Sullivan interjected, his brow furrowed in confusion.

"For years, I lived in Europe, only returning to the United States due to health reasons," Francis explained, her voice steady despite the weight of her words. "While I was in the hospital, a government official made contact with me. Somehow, the information in my medical records triggered a response that I was related to Dr. Zorba. Long story short, the estate was given to me, along with over sixty years of back taxes."

"I had no knowledge of having a great uncle, let alone Dr. Plato Zorba," she continued, her gaze sweeping over the room. "When I was released from the hospital, out of curiosity and the need for money, I sought out the estate. Just the sight of it terrified me, but I mustered up enough courage to enter the mansion. I only lasted one night in the house."

As she finished her tale, Francis turned to establish eye contact with all three occupants in the room. "How old do you think I am?" she asked, her voice quiet but commanding.

"I hesitate to make a guess," Professor Sullivan replied cautiously. "That's one of those loaded questions that could get a man into trouble regardless of how he answers."

"I am only thirty-five years old," Francis revealed, her words hanging heavy in the air. The shock and disbelief were palpable in the room as Sullivan, Nancy, and Stu exchanged incredulous glances.

"That is what one night in the house did to me," Francis concluded, her expression a mask of haunted resolve.

Sullivan is so taken by her story, that, upon reaching for the journals he scatters them over his desktop. As the unsettling silence settled over the room, Francis leaned forward to assist Professor Sullivan in picking up the scattered journals, her movements precise and deliberate. Despite the chaos that had unfolded, she remained stoic, her resolve unshaken in the face of the malevolent forces that lurked within the shadows.

"Professor," Francis's voice cut through the oppressive silence, each word dripping with an eerie sense of urgency. "I'm hoping that you can rid the house of the ghosts that manifest themselves inside so that I can sell the mansion and get on with what life

I have left. I'm prepared to pay you handsomely once you accomplish your task."

Her words hung in the air like a chilling fog, thick and suffocating. The weight of her plea seemed to press down on the room, suffusing the air with an unsettling tension.

Professor Sullivan felt a cold shiver run down his spine as he met Francis's unwavering gaze. There was something unsettling about the way she spoke, a desperate determination that bordered on the edge of madness.

In that moment, the shadows seemed to creep closer, their tendrils reaching out with sinister intent. And as the echoes of her words faded into the darkness, Sullivan couldn't shake the feeling that he had unwittingly stepped into a nightmare from which there may be no escape.

The room remained in a heavy silence, broken only by the soft rustling of Nancy's restless movements in her chair and Stu's incredulous stare fixed on Francis. The discrepancy between her appearance and age hung like a lingering shadow over the room, casting an eerie pallor over the conversation.

At last, it was Professor Sullivan who broke the silence, his voice hesitant yet resolute. "Ms. Zorba, I'm flattered that you reached out to me," he began, his tone weighed down by a sense of responsibility. "But as you mentioned, aside from my academic commitments, my expertise lies in uncovering those who exploit the vulnerable, particularly the elderly or those grieving the loss of a loved one. What you're asking for would require a significant investment of time, resources, and travel, especially considering the remote location of the house in Maine."

Francis remained impassive in the face of Sullivan's refusal, her expression unreadable. Without a word, she reached once again into her purse, producing an overstuffed envelope that landed on Sullivan's desk with a heavy thud. The contents spilled out, revealing a small fortune in crisp $500 bills.

"Here is $25,000 as a retainer," Francis declared, her voice unwavering. "Any additional expenses, whether it be equipment, manpower, or whatever else you require, will be provided without question or justification. My only demand is that the house be cleared of the ghosts that reside within its walls." It was clear that this was no ordinary request, and the stakes were far higher than he could have imagined.

Without a request, she reached out and wrote her phone number on the outside of the envelope. "This is where you can reach me. If you have any questions after you read Dr. Zorba's journals or the events in the house that occurred over sixty-years ago, please contact me." Without waiting for an answer, she stood using the chair as support and gingerly walked to the door. She turned. "Money is no object. It is time for those restless souls to be free."

CHAPTER EIGHT

THE LECTURE HALL crackled with energy as Professor Sullivan concluded his presentation, the image of the imposing façade of the house from the Stephen King movie, "Rose Red," fading from the screen. Murmurs rippled through the room, a mixture of awe and skepticism at the professor's analysis.

"And that concludes our exploration of the quintessential haunted house," Professor Sullivan declared, his voice carrying a note of finality. "What we see in Hollywood may not always reflect the reality of paranormal phenomena, but it certainly shapes our collective imagination. Now, I understand this may be disappointing for some of you, but due to a prior commitment, our next two classes will be conducted remotely."

A ripple of groans and murmurs of discontent echoed through the hall at the news, but Sullivan held up a hand to silence them. "I expect everyone to have their assignments completed on time," he continued, his tone firm. "Excuses such as poor internet connections or Wi-Fi issues will not be accepted. Your responsibility is to ensure that you can participate in our virtual class sessions seamlessly. Thank you."

As the lecture hall began to empty, Stu and Nancy approached Professor Sullivan, accompanied by three new faces. "Professor, this is Tiffany, Thomas, and Jeff," Nancy introduced with a smile. "Each of them comes highly recommended by the IT department and are experts in handling the equipment we'll be using."

Professor Sullivan greeted the newcomers with a nod of acknowledgment, taking note of their eager expressions and the air of competence that surrounded them. With a sense of reassurance in their capabilities, he welcomed them into the fold, recognizing the importance of their expertise in the upcoming endeavor.

With the introductions made, Sullivan gathered his notes and made his way out of the lecture hall, the echo of his footsteps mingling with the lingering buzz of conversation among the students. As he exited, he left behind an atmosphere charged with anticipation and uncertainty, the promise of remote classes signaling a new frontier to navigate in their academic journey.

"Let's head back to my office and go over our agenda. Time is of the essence," Sullivan directed, leading the group as they trailed behind him. As they walked, he took the opportunity to observe the new additions to his investigative team.

Tiffany stood out with her vibrant yellow and pink short hair, adorned with multiple piercings that caught the light as she moved. Despite her slender and wiry frame, there was a palpable energy about her, exuding a bubbly personality that seemed infectious.

Thomas, on the other hand, presented a stark contrast with his muscular build and short-cropped hair. Standing at least 6 feet tall, he exuded a quiet confidence that spoke of years spent in disciplined pursuits. It was clear that he was a man who knew his way around a weight room.

And then there was Jeff, his long blond hair falling delicately around his face in an attempt to conceal his battle with acne. His demeanor was noticeably more reserved, perhaps even shy, as he struggled to maintain eye contact with the others. Of the three, he embodied the stereotype of a computer nerd, his gaze flickering nervously as he adjusted to the presence of his new colleagues.

As they made their way down the hallway, Sullivan couldn't help but ponder the diverse personalities and skill sets that now comprised their team. With such a varied group, each bringing their own strengths and weaknesses to the table, he couldn't help but wonder what challenges lay ahead as they embarked on their investigation into the haunted mansion.

"Pizza should be arriving shortly," Nancy announced, her tone carrying a subtle assertion of her authority within the group. "They'll be bringing sodas, plates, and napkins since I know Professor Sullivan wants this to be a working lunch."

"Absolutely," Sullivan affirmed, nodding in agreement. "Alright everyone, please take a seat so I can connect my laptop to the whiteboard." With a few deft motions, he dimmed the lights in the office and the image of the haunted house flickered to life on the whiteboard.

"Wow, is that the house?" Stu exclaimed, his voice tinged with a mixture of awe and trepidation as everyone leaned in to get a closer look at the imposing facade looming before them.

The mansion stood like a brooding sentinel against the backdrop of the darkening sky, its silhouette looming ominously over the landscape. Its grandeur, once majestic, now marred by the passage of time, was cloaked in an aura of malevolence that seemed to seep from its very foundations.

Towers rose defiantly into the heavens, their jagged spires reaching upward like skeletal fingers grasping at the fading light. Each window, now boarded up or shattered, whispered of untold horrors hidden within, their panes reflecting the twisted shadows that danced in the fading twilight.

Gargoyles adorned the roof line, their grotesque forms frozen in silent screams, their weathered features contorted with anguish. Ivy snaked its way up the crumbling walls, its tendrils weaving a tapestry of decay that seemed to choke the life from the once-majestic structure.

"Yes, these are photos of the house that were included in the journals Ms. Zorba gave me the other day," Sullivan began, his voice carrying a weight of solemnity. "She doesn't know exactly how many rooms are in the house, but believes it is five stories tall. There are several kitchens, bathrooms, and a Victorian-styled conservatory."

Turning his attention to the three new additions to his team, Sullivan continued, "Has Nancy or Stu filled you in about the supposed presence of 13 ghosts in the house?"

Tiffany jumped in eagerly, her eyes alight with excitement. "Yeah, they told us. That's cool. I've always wanted to be inside a haunted house. I visited the Winchester Mystery House in San Jose, and that was unbelievable."

Sullivan glanced at Jeff and Thomas, who nodded in acknowledgment. "Okay then. The following slides are drawings of eleven of the ghosts supposedly that will be our guests when we arrive."

"Only eleven. I thought you said 13, Professor," Thomas asked respectfully, his brow furrowing in confusion.

"All in time, Thomas. All in time," Sullivan replied cryptically, advancing to the next slide. "This is the lion tamer and, of course, the lion. When they manifest themselves, after a few cracks of the bullwhip, the lion tamer attempts to put his head in the lion's mouth. As you can see here, he is never successful."

"Ugh, gross," Tiffany murmured, turning away from the whiteboard, her expression a mixture of fascination and revulsion.

Sullivan clicked forward to the next slide, revealing a chilling tableau. "This is the Italian chef," he began, his voice tinged with a somber tone, "caught in a perpetual cycle of murder within the confines of the kitchen. His victims, his wife and her lover, meet their gruesome fate again and again."

He gestured to the images projected on the screen, each one more haunting than the last. "And here we have the other spirits said to inhabit the house," he continued. "A wailing lady, clutching hands, a fiery skeleton, a hanging lady, an executioner holding a severed head... These drawings are all here in these journals if you would like to see them."

Nancy interjected, her voice cutting through the solemn silence. "If I remember correctly, Ms. Zorba said ghost number twelve was Dr. Plato Zorba, her great uncle, and number thirteen was Benjamin Rush, the shyster lawyer turned murderer."

Sullivan flicked on the lights of his office, casting a warm glow over the room. "Alright, everyone," he began, his tone authoritative yet tinged with a hint of urgency. "Here's a list for each of you. It details personal supplies, food, flashlights, batteries, and anything else we might need."

He distributed the lists to Stu, Thomas, and the rest of the team, watching as they scanned the contents with varying degrees of apprehension. "Stu, I want you and Thomas to take care of gathering the groceries I've listed," he instructed, his gaze settling on the two men. "I'm not sure how long we'll be in the house, but it's better to be overprepared than underprepared. And remember, you can bring your cellphones, but don't count on having any service out there."

As Stu and Thomas nodded in understanding, Sullivan couldn't shake the feeling of unease that lingered in the air. The prospect of venturing into the unknown depths of the haunted mansion weighed heavily on his mind, and he knew that their preparations would be crucial to their survival.

"Alright," Sullivan announced, his voice carrying a note of finality. "After you've completed your assignments, make sure to get a good night's rest. We leave early tomorrow morning at 5 a.m."

He watched as his team members filed out of the office, each one carrying a sense of purpose and determination. As the door closed behind them, Sullivan couldn't help but feel a surge of anticipation mingled with apprehension. Tomorrow would mark the beginning of their journey into the unknown, and he knew that they would need all the rest they could get before facing the mysteries that awaited them in the haunted mansion.

CHAPTER NINE

AS THE NIGHT stretched on, Professor Sullivan found himself tossing and turning in his bed, the weight of impending uncertainty pressing down upon him like a suffocating blanket. Sleep eluded him, the tendrils of restlessness winding their way through his mind.

In the darkness, fragmented images flickered behind closed eyelids, a disjointed montage of memories and dreams. He saw himself behind the wheel of a car, the road stretching out endlessly before him. But there was something wrong, something unsettling about the scene.

In the dream, he was drunk, the world spinning out of control as he struggled to maintain his grip on reality. Panic surged through him as he realized the consequences of his actions, the horror of what was to come looming ever closer.

And then, the crash. The sickening crunch of metal, the screech of tires, the shattering of glass. In an instant, his world shattered, torn apart by the force of impact. His wife, his daughter... gone in an instant, their lives snuffed out by his own recklessness.

Sullivan jolted awake, his heart racing, his body slick with panic sweat. The remnants of the dream clung to him like a sinister fog, casting a pall over his thoughts. But as he struggled to make sense of what he had just experienced, a sense of profound unease settled over him.

He was only married once, divorced long ago with no children to speak of. So why, then, had he dreamt of such a tragedy? Was it merely a trick of the mind, a manifestation of his subconscious fears and anxieties? Or was there something more sinister at play, lurking in the shadows of his own psyche?

As he lay in the darkness, haunted by the echoes of his nightmare, Professor Sullivan couldn't shake the feeling that there were truths hidden beneath the surface, waiting to be unearthed. And as the first light of dawn crept through the window, he knew that the journey into the haunted mansion would bring him face to face with the darkest corners of his own soul.

As Professor Sullivan lay in bed, the weight of his restless thoughts pressing down upon him, his gaze fell upon the box that contained the glasses given to him by Francis Zorba. There was something about it, something inexplicable that drew him in, compelling him to reach out and open it.

He lifted the device from its resting place, marveling at its intricate design and the promise of what it held within. With a sense of anticipation, he unfolded the glasses and placed them on his face, eager to experience the supposed wonders they offered.

At first, his vision was blurred, the world around him swimming in a haze of uncertainty. But then, slowly, things began to come into focus, revealing the familiar objects of his bedroom bathed in an otherworldly light.

Nonsense, he thought, a flicker of disappointment washing over him as he removed the glasses and returned them to their box. With a sigh, he turned off the bedside lamp, plunging the room into darkness once more.

As sleep began to claim him, he paid no heed to the subtle movements of the box on his nightstand, nor the faint whispers that seemed to echo in the silence of the night. Unbeknownst to him, the shadows danced and shifted, a silent specter of the mysteries that lurked just beyond the realm of understanding.

Morning crept over the horizon with an ominous warning, the sky heavy with dark clouds threatening to unleash their fury upon the earth. Professor Sullivan watched from the window as his team gathered by the large van, their figures silhouetted against the backdrop of the looming storm.

"Looks like we're in for some interesting weather," he muttered to himself, a sense of foreboding settling over him like a heavy cloak. The conditions were perfect for a haunted house investigation, he thought grimly, the air crackling with anticipation.

As the team climbed into the van, preparing to embark on their journey into the unknown, Tiffany's voice broke through the tension with a note of levity. "Shouldn't we be playing the theme song to Ghostbusters?" she quipped, a mischievous twinkle in her eye.

The remark elicited laughter from the group, including Professor Sullivan, the tension of the moment momentarily forgotten in the shared moment of humor. But beneath the surface, he couldn't shake the feeling that they were stepping into something far more sinister than a mere ghost hunt.

After a grueling six-hour drive, punctuated only by a handful of bathroom breaks and a hurried lunch, the van finally came to a stop at the base of a looming mountain. There was no address to be seen, no mailbox marking the entrance to their destination. Ms. Zorba had made it clear that the only way to find the correct turnoff was through the use of GPS.

True to her words, the GPS guided them to an overgrown gravel road snaking its way up the hillside, hidden from casual view by the encroaching wilderness. As the van rumbled along the uneven terrain, the sense of isolation grew, the dense foliage closing in around them like the fingers of some unseen specter.

With each passing mile, the air grew thick with anticipation, the weight of their purpose hanging heavy in the air. As they ascended higher into the mountains, Sullivan couldn't shake the feeling that they were venturing into uncharted territory, stepping into a realm where the laws of the mundane world held little sway.

And as the van rounded a bend in the road, revealing the shadowy silhouette of the haunted mansion looming in the distance, a shiver of apprehension ran down his spine. The journey had only just begun, but already, the echoes of the past whispered of the horrors that awaited them within the confines of the house.

"That must be the estate up there," Sullivan remarked, his finger tracing the outline of the summit of the mountain.

"If it looks big from way down here, it must be huge up there," Thomas observed, his voice tinged with a hint of awe.

"Alright, let's take it slow up the road. Doesn't look like anyone has used it in a long, long timc," Sullivan decided, his hands gripping the steering wheel as he prepared to navigate the van along the overgrown path.

Unbeknownst to the four occupants in the back seats, Nancy, feeling a twinge of apprehension, reached out and placed her hand on Sullivan's thigh. She could feel the onset of a panic attack creeping up on her, the weight of the impending unknown bearing down on her with suffocating intensity.

"Listen up, everyone," Sullivan began, his voice carrying a note of authority. "When we arrive, keep in mind that this place has been abandoned for over sixty years. Who knows what kind of damage termites, rats, and roaches have done to the place."

He paused, letting the weight of his words sink in before continuing. "And remember, safety first. We stick together at all times. No wandering off until we get a feel for the place. We'll leave the equipment in the van until we've had a chance to assess the entrance from the inside."

His gaze swept over his team, ensuring that each member understood the gravity of the situation. The air hummed with anticipation, a palpable sense of unease settling over them as they prepared to embark on their investigation.

"Alright, let's do this," Sullivan declared, his voice firm. "Stay alert, stay together, and above all, stay safe." With a sense of determination, the team braced themselves for what lay ahead, knowing that they were venturing into the unknown depths of the abandoned mansion, where secrets and shadows lurked around every corner.

After what felt like an eternity, they finally reached a large wrought iron fence. "Uh oh," Sullivan muttered, a furrow forming on his brow. "Ms. Zorba never said anything about needing a key to the outer fence."

"Yeah. And look at the size of that chain," Jeff said from the back of the van.

Climbing out of the van, Sullivan approached the imposing gate and realized that the padlock was not latched. He removed the lock and began unwrapping the heavy chain. With a determined shove, he pushed the large gate open, its hinges squealing in protest as it reluctantly swung inward. He returned to the van and carefully maneuvered it around a large pond, its surface choked with stagnant water and surrounded by overgrown foliage.

Silently, everyone exited the van, their eyes fixed on the imposing façade of the massive estate. Sullivan led the way, striding ahead of his team until he reached the front door. With a steady hand, he inserted the key into the lock.

The huge double doors creaked open, their rusty hinges protesting against the movement. But what caught Sullivan by surprise was the sound of exhaling gas emanating from the darkness within, as if the very house itself was breathing a sigh of release.

Sullivan turned to his group and noticed that Thomas was still standing by the van, his gaze fixed on the towering structure above. "Thomas, you coming?" Tiffany called out, breaking him from his reverie.

"I just have this feeling like we're being watched," Thomas replied, his tone serious as he scanned the looming façade.

"It's probably just those ugly gargoyles looking down at us," Tiffany said, her laughter cutting through the tension as she grabbed Thomas by the arm and led him towards the entrance.

As they approached, Thomas couldn't shake the unease that lingered in the pit of his stomach. "You know, in all those scary movies I've seen, it's the black guy who always gets it first," he remarked, his voice tinged with apprehension.

"Hey, no one's going to get hurt, Thomas," Sullivan reassured him, his voice steady despite the flickering uncertainty in the air. He tried the light switches, but found them inoperable. With only the faint glow from the open double doors illuminating the entrance hall, Sullivan switched on his flashlight and conducted a thorough sweep of the area.

Directly ahead loomed a massive staircase, its grandeur casting eerie shadows across the room as it ascended to the second floor and branched off in opposing directions. "Don't build homes like this anymore," Stu commented, his voice tinged with a hint of awe and trepidation.

CHAPTER TEN

"LET'S SET UP the generators right outside the entrance so we won't have to worry about exhaust fumes," Sullivan instructed, his voice betraying a hint of unease. "Jeff, while Thomas and Stu are getting the generators ready, bring in the lamps and set them up here. Lastly, we'll bring in all of our monitoring equipment. Ladies, for now, please stay on this floor and stay together."

"Not a problem," Nancy replied quickly, her voice trembling slightly as she and Tiffany turned on their flashlights. But as they moved to comply with Sullivan's instructions, a sudden chill swept through the air, sending shivers down their spines. The front double doors slammed shut.

Everyone froze in their tracks as a ghostly growl echoed from several floors above, the sound reverberating through the ancient halls and sending a primal surge of fear coursing through every cell in their bodies. The air seemed to thicken with malevolent energy, the very atmosphere alive with unseen terrors lurking just beyond the reach of their feeble lights.

In a sudden, eerie twist, the double doors swung open of their own accord, admitting what remained of the afternoon sun into the entrance hall. A tense silence settled over the group as they exchanged wary glances, their attention fixed on Professor Sullivan.

"Don't be alarmed, everyone," Professor Sullivan began, his voice a steadying presence in the midst of the unfolding uncertainty. "As I mentioned earlier, this house has been uninhabited for over sixty years. It's likely that many of the windows are broken, allowing gusts of wind to race through the labyrinth of corridors."

He paused, casting a reassuring glance around the group before continuing. "This could be what caused the double doors to slam shut like that. It's just the elements playing tricks on us." Despite his attempts at reassurance, there was a lingering unease in the air, a sense that they were not alone in the ancient halls of the mansion.

"Remember," Professor Sullivan reiterated, his voice calm but firm. "Houses breathe. They react to atmospheric pressures, fluctuations in temperature, and the natural ebb and flow of their surroundings. Factor in corroded pipes, trapped gas in the sewer lines, and who knows what else, and you have a recipe for all sorts of strange phenomena. But rest assured, everything can be explained."

As he spoke, he made a conscious effort to instill a sense of rationality in his team, hoping to dispel any lingering sense of fear or unease that might be creeping into their minds. Yet, even as he spoke the words, Sullivan couldn't shake the feeling that there was more to this place than met the eye, that perhaps some mysteries were best left unsolved.

"Now, I don't know about the rest of you, but I'm hungry. The faster we can set up our gear and get are camping stove working, the faster we can get some food cooking."

"Sounds good to me, Professor, said Thomas as he and Stu went out of the house and started carrying the first of several generators. As Nancy and Tiffany continued to search the first floor, they arrived at what they believed was a large library.

"Look at that guy over the fireplace," Nancy remarked, directing the beam of her flashlight towards a large portrait hanging above the mantelpiece. The figure depicted a stern-looking man dressed in a turn-of-the-century suit. "I wonder if that's old Dr. Plato Zorba, the great occultist?"

"Whoever it is, it gives me the creeps," Tiffany responded, her voice tinged with unease. She turned her attention to the hallway beside them, the narrow passage stretching out before them like a yawning abyss. "And this hallway... it's just... weird."

Nancy joined her, their combined flashlight beams slicing through the darkness. Yet, despite their efforts, the hallway seemed to extend endlessly into the shadows, its secrets hidden in the depths beyond.

"Look at the writing over this door," Nancy said, her voice trembling as she pointed her flashlight towards the intricate symbols etched into the ancient wood. "I've never seen anything like that before."

Tiffany reached out tentatively, her fingers tracing the twisted lines of the writing. But as she pulled her hand away, she gasped in horror, her breath catching in her throat. "Oh, God. I must be cut," she exclaimed, panic rising in her voice as she stared at the crimson stains on her fingertips.

"Let me see," Nancy said, her heart pounding with fear as she reached for Tiffany's hand. But when she examined Tiffany's fingers, there was nothing there, no trace of blood to be found. She looked up in confusion, her eyes meeting Tiffany's shocked gaze.

"What the hell? They were covered in blood, I swear," Tiffany insisted, her voice trembling with disbelief as she continued to examine her fingertips, searching desperately for an explanation.

"We need to get back to the others," Nancy said, her tone urgent as she grabbed Tiffany's hand and pulled her away from the door. As they hurried down the hallway, the door they had just left creaked open slowly, as if beckoning them back into the darkness. Then, with a sudden shudder, it slammed shut behind them, sealing off the room with an ominous finality.

As Nancy and Tiffany stepped into the grand entrance, now bathed in artificial light from the lamps Jeff had set up powered by the hum of the generator outside, Sullivan glanced up and greeted them with a smile. "Right on time, ladies," he said warmly. "It's nothing fancy, but we've got hot dogs, BBQ beans, and rolls almost ready. Everyone, grab a plate and utensils and dig in." With a wave of his hand, he gestured towards the makeshift dining area, inviting his team to partake in the simple meal.

As dinner came to a close, Nancy found a moment to pull Professor Sullivan aside, her expression serious as she spoke in hushed tones. "Professor, I need to talk to you about something," she began, her voice filled with a sense of urgency.

Sullivan's brow furrowed with concern as he turned his attention to Nancy. "Of course, what's on your mind?" he inquired, his curiosity piqued by her demeanor.

With a glance around to ensure they wouldn't be overheard, Nancy leaned in closer, her voice dropping to a whisper. "It's about Tiffany," she confessed, her tone tinged with unease. "She witnessed something down that hallway just before we ate."

Sullivan's interest was immediately piqued. "What did she see?" he asked, leaning in closer to catch every word.

Nancy hesitated, choosing her words carefully before relaying what Tiffany had experienced. "She's a little embarrassed and doesn't want to share all the details," she admitted. "But she felt you should be aware. It could be nothing, just a trick of the mind after the long drive we all endured, but I thought it best to let you know."

After a brief pause, Nancy pressed on. "We decided to explore that hallway over there together," she recounted, her voice tinged with apprehension. "That's when we stumbled upon some strange markings etched into the door frame. Tiffany, curious as ever, ran her fingertips over the writing. To our horror, she saw blood, but when she turned to show me, there was nothing there."

CHAPTER ELEVEN

"Consider this, Nancy," Sullivan murmured, his voice barely above a whisper, "I'm not discounting Tiffany's perception of what she claims to have seen. The human mind possesses an extraordinary ability to conjure illusions, especially under conditions of fatigue and stress. After enduring a prolonged journey, the mind can play tricks, weaving shadows into apparitions, and transforming ordinary sights into spectral visions." He glanced toward Tiffany, her expression still unsettled from the encounter. "Exhaustion has a way of distorting reality, planting seeds of the uncanny where none truly exist."

""Alright, team," Professor Sullivan addressed the group, his voice carrying authority softened by a tinge of anticipation. "We owe a debt of gratitude to Thomas and Stu for getting the generators up and running. Jeff, excellent work on the lighting setup. And let's not forget our indispensable ladies, who have graciously taken care of our dinner necessities."

He surveyed the assembled group, ensuring everyone was attentive before continuing. "Now, before we retire for the evening, I propose we take advantage of our newfound illumination and explore this floor of the estate. But let's proceed cautiously and stick together. Make certain your flashlights are in working order and remain vigilant."

With a glance toward the old journals in his possession, Sullivan's eyes gleamed with scholarly curiosity. "According to the writings of Dr. Plato Zorba, our first destination holds the legend of the hanging woman. Intriguing, isn't it?" He paused, a faint smile playing at the corners of his lips. "Let's see what secrets this estate holds within its walls."

Sullivan cradled the purportedly mystical lenses in his grasp, concealing within his jacket pocket a 9mm semi-automatic, a secret arsenal unbeknownst to the rest of the group. His gaze flicked over a map meticulously sketched by Dr. Zorba, a guide to the ethereal labyrinth they found themselves in. With a momentary pause to orient himself, Sullivan's index finger traced a path on the map, diverging from the well-trodden route previously ventured by Nancy and Tiffany.

As the group prepared to depart from the grand entrance hall, Tiffany's sudden announcement of her forgotten purse brought their progress to an abrupt halt. With murmurs of understanding, they watched as she retraced her steps into the main foyer, disappearing momentarily from view.

But as Tiffany's figure vanished into the shadows of the foyer, a subtle unease settled over the remaining members of the group. Without warning, the massive chandelier suspended above the room began to sway ominously, its once-stationary form now trembling with an eerie rhythm. A collective gasp escaped the lips of the onlookers as fissures appeared in the ceiling, shedding flakes of plaster and debris to the floor below.

Nancy's voice pierced through the mounting tension, her urgent cry echoing in the cavernous space. "Tiffany, run!" she shouted, her words laced with a desperate plea. Reacting instinctively to the imminent danger, Tiffany bolted forward just as the chandelier plummeted from its perch, crashing violently onto the polished marble floor mere inches behind her fleeing form. With a thunderous roar, shards of glass and metal erupted outward, scattering across the foyer in a deadly dance of destruction.

Nancy's voice rang out in a mixture of horror and relief as she sprinted toward Tiffany, enveloping her friend in a tight embrace. "Thank God you're safe!" she exclaimed, her heart still racing from the adrenaline-fueled escape.

"As I've been emphasizing," Sullivan interjected, his tone measured yet authoritative, "we must exercise extreme caution as we continue our exploration. It's abundantly clear that this house is in a state of severe disrepair." Casting a reassuring glance at the group, he gestured toward the hallway ahead. "Let's proceed with care. Follow in the footsteps of the person before you, maintaining a slow and deliberate pace."

With a nod of determination, Sullivan led the way forward, his movements deliberate as he navigated the dimly lit corridor. Each step reverberated through the ancient floorboards, a reminder of the precarious nature of their surroundings. As the group pressed onward, their senses heightened, attuned to the slightest shift in the atmosphere as they delved deeper into the heart of the haunted estate.

"Professor, why did this Dr. Plato Zorba build such a large mansion?" Thomas asked, his gaze drifting down the seemingly endless hallway.

"I had to do some Internet searches to get that information, since Ms. Francis Zorba did not include that in her discussion of the house," Professor Sullivan replied, adjusting his glasses. "It seems that Dr. Zorba was born into old money. He had all the finer things in life except for a wife and hopes of a large family."

"Ah," Nancy interjected, prompting smiles from the group.

"He found the most beautiful woman in Chicago and after a whirlwind romance, married her. That is when he bought this large acreage and began supervising the construction of the estate. He desired a large family, so right from the start his plans were for a grand home."

"His wife unfortunately had two miscarriages, but on their third attempt, a daughter, April, was born. Sadly, she died four days later. The doctor informed his wife that she would not be able to become pregnant again. Shortly thereafter, his wife died."

"How did she die?" Tiffany inquired, her voice tinged with curiosity.

"In all of my research, it never listed her cause of death. Apparently, however, that was the trigger for Dr. Zorba to delve deeply into the occult," Professor Sullivan explained.

"Sorry. I think there is more to the story about this place," Tiffany said, her uneasiness palpable.

As the group ventured further into the bowels of the decrepit mansion, the air grew thick with an oppressive weight, suffused with a palpable sense of foreboding. With each step, the ancient floorboards creaked and groaned beneath their feet, echoing through the shadowy corridors like mournful whispers from the past. The flickering light cast by their flashlights danced eerily across the peeling wallpaper, conjuring grotesque shadows that seemed to writhe and twist in the dimness.

Suddenly, amid the oppressive silence, a low, guttural groan echoed through the darkness, causing everyone to freeze. It was followed by a chilling chorus of ghoulish laughter, echoing from unseen corners of the house like the sinister cackle of malevolent spirits. The hair on the back of their necks stood on end as the unearthly sounds reverberated through the halls, freezing them in their tracks.

As the echoes of laughter faded into the oppressive silence, a blood-curdling scream pierced the air, tearing through the stillness with its raw intensity. The group recoiled in terror, their hearts pounding in their chests as they exchanged fearful glances. "Is that the house too?" Thomas stammered, his voice trembling with fear as he struggled to mask his mounting terror. His question a stark reminder of the unseen horrors lurking within the walls of the haunted estate.

With each passing moment, the oppressive atmosphere seemed to close in around them, suffocating them with its malevolent presence. The air grew thick with dread as they stood paralyzed, uncertain of what terrors awaited them in the darkness. With nerves stretched to the breaking point, they braced themselves for whatever horrors lay ahead, steeling their resolve to confront the unknown with unwavering determination.

Professor Sullivan stepped forward, his voice calm yet tinged with a hint of skepticism as he attempted to rationalize the unsettling phenomena that had just unfolded before them. "Now, now, let's not jump to conclusions," he began, his tone measured as he addressed the group. "It's entirely possible that what we just heard was nothing more than the natural sounds of an old house settling."

He gestured towards the crumbling walls and sagging ceilings surrounding them. "These old estates are often filled with all manner of creaks and groans as the wood expands and contracts with the changing temperature," he explained, his words echoing through the dimly lit corridor. "And as for the laughter and screams, well, our minds can sometimes play tricks on us, especially in environments as... atmospheric as this."

Despite his attempts at reassurance, Sullivan couldn't shake the unease that lingered in the pit of his stomach. The rational explanations he offered felt hollow in the face of the palpable sense of dread that hung heavy in the air. But he pressed on, determined to maintain a facade of composure in the face of mounting uncertainty.

"Let's press on, shall we?" Sullivan suggested, forcing a smile as he motioned for the group to continue. "There's no need to let our imaginations get the better of us. We have a job to do, after all." And with that, he led the way forward, his footsteps echoing through the haunted halls as they plunged deeper into the heart of the estate, each step bringing them closer to the truth... and to the unknown horrors that awaited them. Professor Sullivan stepped forward, his voice calm yet tinged with a hint of skepticism as he attempted to rationalize the unsettling phenomena that had just unfolded before them. "Now, now, let's not jump to conclusions," he began, his tone measured as he addressed the group. "It's entirely possible that what we just heard was nothing more than the natural sounds of an old house settling."

He gestured towards the crumbling walls and sagging ceilings surrounding them. "These old estates are often filled with all manner of creaks and groans as the wood expands and contracts with the changing temperature," he explained, his words echoing through the dimly lit corridor. "And as for the laughter and screams, well, our minds can sometimes play tricks on us, especially in environments as... atmospheric as this."

Despite his attempts at reassurance, Sullivan couldn't shake the unease that lingered in the pit of his stomach. The rational explanations he offered felt hollow in the face of the palpable sense of dread that hung heavy in the air. But he pressed on, determined to maintain a facade of composure in the face of mounting uncertainty. He felt his weapon which gave him some relief.

CHAPTER TWELVE

SULLIVAN PAUSED BEFORE a weathered door, his gaze flitting between the faded pages of an old journal and the worn wood before him. "I do believe we've reached our destination," he remarked, his voice carrying a note of uncertainty as he relayed the sparse information gleaned from the journal's yellowed pages. "There's little to be said about the occupant of this chamber, save for Dr. Plato Zorba's cryptic notation of her tragic demise in a Parisian room, where she met her end by her own hand. No motive, no background—merely a number assigned to her: number 1 and the name 'Hanging woman.'"

With a steady hand, Sullivan tested the door's knob, finding it surprisingly unlocked. As he eased the door open, a chill wind rushed forth flooding the hallway. The door resisted his efforts, as if reluctant to reveal the secrets concealed within. With a determined push, Sullivan finally succeeded in swinging the door wide, illuminating the chamber beyond with the beam of his flashlight.

Victorian-era furnishings greeted his gaze, draped in layers of dust and cobwebs that spoke of decades of neglect. A four-poster bed stood sentinel in the center of the room, its linens still pristine despite the passage of time. But there were no signs of life within, no whisper of movement to disturb the silence that hung heavy in the air. As Sullivan stepped further into the room, he couldn't shake the feeling of being watched, as if the very walls themselves held secrets waiting to be uncovered.

As Sullivan ventured further into the room, an unsettling sensation washed over him, a feeling of being watched by unseen eyes that lurked in the shadows. He couldn't shake the feeling that the walls themselves held secrets waiting to be uncovered, their ancient whispers echoing through the darkness, beckoning him deeper into the heart of the haunted estate.

"Maybe you should use the special glasses," Nancy suggested from the hallway, her voice trembling with a mixture of curiosity and apprehension.

Sullivan nodded in agreement, his movements deliberate as he reached into the pocket opposite his concealed weapon. With a sense of cautious anticipation, he withdrew the special spectacles and carefully positioned them on his head, adjusting them until they rested comfortably over his eyes. Peering back into the dimly lit room, he strained to discern any sign of the purported apparition.

As another groan echoed from within the chamber, Sullivan's focus sharpened, his gaze intent on unraveling the mystery before him. Yet, before he could make sense of the situation, the door slammed shut behind him with a resounding thud, sealing him off from the rest of the group.

Sullivan grabbed the door handle and tried to open it. It would not turn. Still wearing the glasses he turned feeling a cold wind on his shoulders. Nothing was there.

Outside, Nancy and the others strained against the unyielding door, their efforts met with frustration as it remained firmly locked, trapping Sullivan within the mysterious room. With mounting concern etched upon their faces, they exchanged worried glances, their anxiety growing with each passing moment as they awaited any sign of their colleague's fate.

Meanwhile, inside the chamber, Sullivan adjusted the focus of the glasses with a sense of urgency, his gaze sweeping over the room in search of any elusive specter. Yet, despite his best efforts, the scene before him remained unchanged, devoid of the ghostly apparition they had hoped to uncover. Frustration mingled with disappointment as he removed the glasses, the weight of failure heavy upon his shoulders.

As if in response to his actions, the door to the room swung open with a suddenness that startled him. Startled, he stepped back, his gaze meeting Nancy's concerned eyes as she peered into the room.

"Professor, are you alright?" she inquired, her voice tinged with worry.

"We tried everything to open the door," Thomas interjected, his brow furrowed with exertion as he wiped sweat from his forehead. "But it was like trying to move a mountain. The harder we pushed, the harder it pushed back." His words hung in the air, a testament to the inexplicable forces at play within the haunted confines of the estate.

"I'm fine," Sullivan reassured them with a smile, though a hint of disappointment flickered in his eyes. "Unfortunately, even with the glasses, there was no sign of a ghost inside." He sighed softly, acknowledging the dashed hopes of uncovering the paranormal.

Glancing at his watch, Sullivan's expression turned thoughtful. "It's growing late, and we've got a lot more of this house to explore tomorrow," he remarked. "I suggest we each find a room nearby and call it a night." He paused, his gaze sweeping over the weary faces of his companions. "We'll regroup in the morning, refreshed and ready to tackle whatever mysteries this place has in store for us."

With a nod of agreement, the group began to disperse, each member seeking out a room to rest in for the night. As they retreated into the darkness of the sprawling estate, the echoes of their footsteps mingled with the whispers of the past, a reminder of the haunted history that awaited them with the dawn of a new day.

Upon spotting the room Sullivan had settled on for the night, Nancy made a point of selecting the adjacent quarters, ensuring their proximity for safety and support. With each member choosing a room neighboring the others, they exchanged friendly goodnight wishes, their voices echoing softly in the dimly lit hallway.

As the group dispersed into their respective rooms, the sound of locking doors reverberated through the corridor, a chorus of security measures to ward off the lingering unease of the haunted estate. Alone in his chosen room, Sullivan surveyed the furnishings, noting their resemblance to the chamber where he had been briefly trapped earlier. With a determined resolve, he set about making the space his own, discarding the dust-covered bed coverings and arranging his sleeping bag and pillow on the mattress.

With a weary sigh, Sullivan settled onto the makeshift bed, Dr. Zorba's journal clasped in his hands. The weight of the day's events hung heavy upon him as he turned the pages, the flickering lamplight casting eerie shadows across the worn pages. Yet, despite the oppressive atmosphere of the haunted mansion, he found a sense of solace in the familiarity of the journal's pages, each word a beacon of knowledge in the midst of the unknown.

As Sullivan delved into Dr. Plato Zorba's journal, his interest increased with each page turn. The meticulous descriptions of spectral encounters and the painstakingly documented backgrounds of each trapped ghost held his attention captive, confirming the stories Francis Zorba had shared during their earlier conversation. Yet, as he reached the final entry and closed the journal, a nagging doubt crept into his mind.

Was it possible that this elaborate tale of ghostly hauntings was merely a ruse concocted by Francis Zorba? Had she orchestrated this entire charade with the intention of capitalizing on the reputation of Sullivan and his team? The notion lingered in the back of his mind, casting a shadow of suspicion over their mission to uncover the truth behind the purported haunting of the estate.

Sullivan weighed the evidence before him, grappling with the unsettling possibility that they had been deceived. As he contemplated the implications of Francis Zorba's motives, a sense of unease settled over him, prompting him to approach their investigation with renewed caution and skepticism. After all, in the shadowy world of the paranormal, not everything was as it seemed.

CHAPTER THIRTEEN

THROUGHOUT THE NIGHT, the eerie sounds of groans, screams, and howling wind persisted within the confines of the mansion. Despite the unsettling atmosphere, neither Professor Sullivan nor any of his students dared to venture beyond the safety of their locked rooms. Despite the unnerving cacophony echoing through the halls, they found a semblance of security within the confines of their chambers.

The next morning, Sullivan took the initiative to break the tense silence, emerging from his room and traversing the dimly lit hallway. With each door he reached, he gently roused his fellow companions, uniting them one by one until all six stood together in the corridor. Together, they made their way to the nearest kitchen, where Nancy and Tiffany wasted no time in springing into action, swiftly preparing breakfast to chase away the lingering shadows of the night.

"Professor," Jeff inquired, his voice laced with curiosity, "were you aware of the myriad sounds echoing through the house from your room?"

Sullivan paused, savoring a sip of his coffee before replying, "Indeed, Jeff. I suspect we all bore witness to those unsettling sounds. Yet, considering the vast age of this estate, who can truly discern their origins?"

Thomas, unconvinced by Sullivan's response, pressed further. "Professor, forgive my persistence, but Tiffany, Jeff, and I lack the privilege of attending your psychology classes. Would you be willing to enlighten us on your skepticism regarding the existence of ghosts?"

"A ghost, according to popular belief, is the spirit of a deceased individual who, for reasons unknown, chooses not to depart to the afterlife and instead remains on the earthly plane after the death of their physical body. It's important to note that such occurrences are exceptionally rare."

"These spirits are not tethered to any specific location on Earth, but they often gravitate towards places they once knew or frequented in life. If the place they inhabit is destroyed or altered, the spirit may relocate to another earthly location or ultimately return to their home in the spirit world. Upon returning to the spirit realm, they undergo a period of learning and are granted the ability to return to Earth at will, where they can stay for as long as they desire."

"Many choose to revisit Earth to reconnect with loved ones, a practice that occurs frequently and often without the awareness of those who remain behind. This interpretation is widely accepted among parapsychologists and occultists." He took another sip of his coffee and could tell that not only Thomas who asked the question, but Tiffany and Jeff were hanging on each of his words.

"At times, a spirit may choose to linger if they pass away in a place they hold dear, or if they are reluctant to part from loved ones, particularly if the death was sudden or traumatic. Regardless of the circumstances, as time passes and the living move forward with their lives, the spirit remains tethered to the earthly realm."

"They become energetically 'stuck,' unable to perceive the guiding light that leads souls to the afterlife. This phenomenon is akin to how one may not always notice light in their daily surroundings. Here, spiritualists offer their assistance. For a fee, they guide these lingering spirits towards the light, assuring them that it is safe to move on."

Sullivan paused, his gaze sweeping over the group gathered before him. "Forgive me, I seem to have slipped into lecturer mode," he apologized.

"No need to apologize, Professor. Please, continue. I find this truly fascinating," Tiffany urged, her curiosity mirrored by the nods of encouragement from the rest of the group, including Nancy and Stu, who had heard Sullivan's lectures on numerous occasions.

"Understand that when individuals undergo what is termed a 'difficult death,' their spirits can sometimes become ensnared in the 'Middle World,' the realm where we reside and carry out our daily lives," Sullivan resumed. "There are various reasons for this occurrence. A spirit may be confused at the moment of passing, unaware of their own demise and unable to find their way into the guiding light."

"Alternatively," he continued, "a spirit may harbor a sense of possessiveness towards their former dwelling, feeling aggrieved by the intrusion of new occupants and compelled to linger in order to protect what they perceive as their space. Being trapped in the Middle World can be a distressing and disorienting experience for these spirits, compounded by feelings of revenge, anger, or profound emotional attachment."

"In such cases," Sullivan elaborated, "the effects of a haunting can manifest in numerous ways. From strange smells and moving objects to eerie voices and sensations of being watched, the signs of a haunting can be unmistakable. Electrical malfunctions, gas leaks, and plumbing issues may also plague the premises, along with a pervasive sense of unease and coldness."

"Last night's experiences seem to tie in with what we've discussed," Thomas interjected, prompting nods of agreement from the group.

Tiffany and Nancy's screams pierced the air, echoing through the vast halls of the mansion as a deafening crash shattered the silence, emanating from the cavernous grand entrance. With trepidation clawing at their senses, they trailed behind Sullivan, their hearts pounding in their chests, drawn inexorably to the source of the disturbance.

Upon reaching the grand entrance, a chill settled over the group as they beheld the scene before them. Equipment lay strewn across the marble floor, scattered like discarded relics of some forgotten experiment. Nancy's hands trembled as she reached out to touch a fallen device, her fingers recoiling at the icy chill that seemed to seep from its metal casing.

"More wind, Professor?" Thomas's voice dripped with skepticism, a thin veil of disbelief masking his unease. But Sullivan offered no reply, his gaze fixated on the desolate expanse of the room, a sense of foreboding clinging to the empty space like a shroud.

In the dim light filtering through the stained glass windows, shadows danced ominously along the walls, twisting and contorting into grotesque shapes that seemed to leer malevolently at the intruders. A faint whispering filled the air, indiscernible words carrying on a ghostly breeze that sent shivers cascading down their spines.

As Sullivan stooped to retrieve the fallen equipment, a sudden gust of frigid air rushed through the entrance, extinguishing the feeble glow of their flashlights and plunging the room into darkness. In that moment of utter blackness, a sense of profound dread descended upon them, suffocating and oppressive, as if the very walls of the mansion were closing in around them.

With trembling hands, everyone shook their flashlights in a desperate attempt to coax forth the comforting glow of illumination. But the darkness clung to the room like a malevolent specter, refusing to yield to their feeble efforts.

Suddenly, in the heart of the chamber, a ghastly figure materialized before their horrified eyes. It was the apparition of the 'hanging woman,' her spectral form hovering ominously above the ground. No words escaped her pallid lips, only a haunting silence as she lingered like a wraith for a fleeting moment, before vanishing into the very fabric of the ceiling.

Terror gripped the group in its icy grasp, freezing them in place as the echoes of Tiffany's panicked screech pierced the air. "I'm out of here!" she cried, her voice tinged with raw fear as she made a frantic dash towards the double entry doors.

But her path to escape was thwarted; the doors, once within reach, now seemed to elude her grasp, mocking her futile attempts to flee. Panic surged through her veins as she pounded on the unyielding wood, pleading for release from this nightmare.

Thomas, sensing her mounting terror, rushed to her side, his own fear palpable in the air. "I'm with you, sis," he declared, his voice trembling as he joined her futile efforts to force open the doors.

As their desperation reached a fever pitch, a chilling laughter reverberated through the silent halls of the mansion, an unholy sound that seemed to emanate from the very walls themselves. It echoed with a sinister promise, a grim reminder that they were not alone in this house of horrors.

CHAPTER FOURTEEN

SULLIVAN AND THE rest of the group rushed to reunite with Thomas and Tiffany, their footsteps echoing loudly in the oppressive silence of the grand entrance. As Sullivan attempted to pry open the stubborn doors to no avail, he could feel the rising tide of panic engulfing the group, their fear palpable in the air like a suffocating fog.

Sullivan took a deep breath, his mind racing for words to soothe their frayed nerves. "Listen, everyone," he began, his voice steady despite the tremor of unease that lingered beneath the surface. "I know this is terrifying, but we need to stay calm. Panicking won't help us get out of here. We need to think clearly and rationally."

He glanced around at the group, meeting each of their frightened gazes with a reassuring nod. "We're in this together, and we'll find a way out. Let's focus on finding another exit or a way to signal for help. We're not alone, and we will get through this," he declared, his words carrying a quiet strength that began to ease the tension in the room.

As the group huddled together, their fear slowly gave way to a glimmer of hope, fueled by Sullivan's unwavering resolve. In the face of the unknown horrors that lurked within the mansion's walls, they found solace in their unity and determination to overcome whatever darkness awaited them.

Nancy broke the heavy silence that hung over the group. "Professor, you saw the ghost just like the rest of us, right?" Sullivan nodded in confirmation. She turned her gaze to the others gathered around her. "And all of us saw her too?" she queried, prompting a chorus of nods from the group.

"But here's the thing," Nancy continued, furrowing her brow in confusion. "None of us were wearing those special glasses. So how did we all see the 'hanging lady'?"

Sullivan felt the weight of Nancy's question settle upon him, a heavy burden demanding a response. His mind raced, searching for a rational explanation to offer the group, but he found himself at a loss. Despite his training and experience in matters of the supernatural, the appearance of the ghostly apparition defied any logical explanation he could conjure.

He took a moment to gather his thoughts, his brow furrowed in concentration as he grappled with the unsettling reality of what they had witnessed. None of his textbooks or lectures had prepared him for such a phenomenon, and the absence of the special glasses only deepened the mystery.

"I…I'm not entirely sure," Sullivan began slowly, his voice betraying his uncertainty. "What we saw…it defies any conventional explanation. It's as if…as if the veil between our world and the realm of the spirits has been momentarily lifted."

He glanced around at the group, his eyes meeting theirs in shared bewilderment. "Perhaps…perhaps there are forces at play here that we simply do not yet understand," he ventured, his words tinged with a sense of resignation. "But rest assured, we will do everything in our power to unravel this mystery and find a way out of here."

With a sense of resolve, Sullivan stepped forward, reclaiming a semblance of authority amidst the swirling chaos. He made his way to the table where the group's equipment lay strewn, his fingers searching through the clutter until they found what he sought. Among the items, his touch met several candles, their wicks waiting patiently for the spark of a flame.

Taking a deep breath, Sullivan struck a match, its tiny flame dancing to life as he brought it to the waiting candles. The room flickered with the warm glow of candlelight, casting long shadows that danced along the walls like specters of the night. In the gentle illumination, a sense of calm descended upon the group, a temporary respite from the encroaching darkness.

But as Sullivan passed the candles to each member of the group, their hands closing around the flickering flames, a strange phenomenon unfolded before their eyes. One by one, their flashlights, previously dormant, sprang to life, casting aside the need for the candles as beams of light pierced the darkness once more.

A collective gasp filled the room as the candles were rendered obsolete, their once comforting glow now overshadowed by the harsh brilliance of the flashlights. Sullivan's brow furrowed in confusion as he surveyed the scene before him, grappling with the inexplicable twist of fate that had unfolded in their midst.

"I need the men to circle around the grand entrance," Sullivan directed, his voice steady despite the tension that hung in the air like a thick fog. "Tear down those worn curtains and check each window. We're searching for one that's sturdy enough to be smashed, giving us a way out of here."

His words carried a sense of urgency, a stark reminder of their precarious situation. With determined nods, the male members of the group sprang into action, their movements purposeful as they set about their task. Each torn curtain revealed a window, their frames weathered by time and neglect, yet offering a glimmer of hope for escape amidst the looming shadows of the mansion.

With haste, the males obeyed Sullivan's command, their movements swift yet fraught with apprehension.

Thomas, his hands trembling with adrenaline, seized a nearby chair and hurled it towards a looming stained glass window, the impact echoing through the chamber like a mournful lament. But to their horror, the chair rebounded off the window's surface with an eerie resilience, leaving the glass unmarred and unyielding.

Undeterred by the failure, Sullivan and Stu followed suit, each selecting a different window and unleashing their desperate fury upon it. Yet, to their dismay, the results remained unchanged, as the windows defied their efforts with an unnatural resistance, mocking their attempts at escape.

As the futile assault unfolded before their eyes, Tiffany and Nancy could feel the tendrils of panic tightening around their hearts, their screams of terror swallowed by the oppressive silence of the mansion. In the face of such unrelenting darkness, their hope began to wane, replaced by a creeping dread that threatened to consume them whole.

Sullivan's frustration simmered beneath the surface as their attempts to break through the windows yielded no success. With a clenched jaw and furrowed brow, he felt the weight of responsibility pressing down upon him, the pressure of leadership bearing heavily upon his shoulders.

"Damn it!" Sullivan exclaimed, his voice laced with frustration, his hands balling into fists at his sides. But as quickly as his anger flared, he took a deep breath, his features softening into a mask of determination.

"We will find a way out of here," he declared, his tone firm and unwavering. "We just need to keep our heads clear and work together. There has to be another way."

With renewed resolve, Sullivan rallied the group, leading them once more into the depths of the mansion's main floor. As they ventured forth, the dim light of their flashlights casting eerie shadows along the corridor walls, Sullivan retrieved Dr. Zorba's journals once again, his fingers tracing the worn pages in search of answers amidst the cryptic passages.

Together, they resumed their search through the rooms and corridors, their footsteps echoing in the empty halls as they delved deeper into the secrets that lay hidden within the mansion's walls. With each turn of the page and each step forward, they drew closer to uncovering the truth behind their haunting predicament, their determination unwavering in the face of the unknown horrors that awaited them.

"This room is said to house the ghost of 'flaming swords,' whatever that entails," Sullivan remarked, his tone tinged with skepticism as he swung open the door and peered into the room, the special glasses perched upon his nose. But once again, the room remained empty, devoid of any spectral presence.

"Enough of this," Sullivan declared, his frustration palpable as he removed the glasses and turned to face the group. "I'm not sure what kind of game is being played here, but out of the supposed thirteen ghosts haunting this house, we've only encountered one. It's time we seek answers elsewhere."

With a determined stride, Sullivan led the group towards the library, his mind buzzing with the possibility of finding a clue or solution hidden amidst the dusty tomes and ancient manuscripts that lined the shelves. It was their best chance at unraveling the mysteries of the mansion and finding a means of escape from its sinister clutches.

CHAPTER FIFTEEN

"THAT'S THE PICTURE Nancy and I saw earlier," Tiffany remarked, her voice tinged with unease as the group entered the library and dispersed among the shelves.

Sullivan approached the fireplace, drawn to the portrait hanging above it—an ominous depiction of the enigmatic occultist, old man Zorba. As he studied the painting, a sense of foreboding settled over him, the eyes of the portrait seeming to follow his every move.

Meanwhile, Thomas, Jeff, and Stu directed their attention to the wall adorned with several windows, their gazes lingering on the glass panes with apprehension. Despite the urgency of their situation, they hesitated to attempt breaking through them, a lingering sense of dread whispering caution in their ears.

As Sullivan studied the portrait of old man Zorba, a chilling curiosity seized him, compelling him to don the special glasses once more. As the lenses obscured his vision, a low, guttural groan emanated from the picture, sending a shiver down his spine. Yet, to his dismay, no spectral manifestation materialized before him, leaving him feeling frustrated and disheartened.

With a disgusted huff, Sullivan removed the glasses and flung them onto the fireplace mantle, his hopes of uncovering answers fading like wisps of smoke. To his astonishment, as the glasses clattered against the stone, a hidden mechanism within the mantle was triggered, causing part of the library's shelves to slide apart with a soft click.

"Stand back, everybody," Professor Sullivan commanded, his voice firm with authority. "Let me go in there alone so no one gets hurt." With cautious steps, he advanced towards the dark hidden room, his flashlight piercing the thick shadows. The anticipation hung heavy in the air as his team waited anxiously outside.

Sullivan estimated the room to be approximately 8 feet wide and 12 feet long. As he entered, he felt a shiver crawl down his spine, the darkness seeming to press in on him from all sides. There were no shelves, only blank walls closing in around him. The smell of mold permeated the enclosure, assaulting his senses.

He turned back to his waiting group, his face barely visible in the dim light. "Looks like another wild goose chase," he muttered, disappointment evident in his voice. But he wasn't ready to give up just yet. With determination, he began to explore, his footsteps echoing in the eerie silence.

Pounding on the walls, Sullivan listened intently as each thump reverberated through the chamber, the sound bouncing off the walls and echoing back to him from the library beyond. His heart raced as he continued, searching for any sign of a clue or hidden passage.

Then, as his hand connected with the back wall, he felt it give way slightly. With a surge of excitement, he pushed harder, and to his amazement, the top portion of the wall began to rise, revealing a small cabinet hidden within. And there, lying innocuously on top of the cabinet, was a single item: a weathered notebook.

"I've found something," Sullivan exclaimed, his voice tinged with excitement and curiosity, as he emerged from the hidden room and rejoined the waiting group. "It looks like a diary."

"Whose diary?" an impatient Nancy inquired, her curiosity piqued.

With careful hands, Sullivan wiped off layers of dust and cobwebs, revealing in elegant gold lettering on the front cover: The Diary of Ann Zorba.

A smile spread across Sullivan's face as he held up the diary triumphantly. "It's Ann Zorba's diary," he announced, his satisfaction evident in his tone. This could be the key to unlocking the mysteries of the house and the Zorba family."

He turned to the first page, put on his reading glasses, and read it to the group.

"April, 5, 1959"

Dear Diary,

Today marks another year of my marriage with Plato. Oh, how fortunate I am to have him as my husband. From the moment we exchanged vows, I knew that our love was destined to withstand the test of time. His intellect, charm, and unwavering devotion make every day a joyous celebration of our union.

I find myself reflecting on the early days of our courtship, when every stolen glance and tender caress filled my heart with overwhelming happiness. Together, we dreamed of building a future filled with love, laughter, and the pitter-patter of little feet.

However, as time passed, our dreams were tempered by the harsh reality of life's challenges. The pain of our first miscarriage tested our resolve but only strengthened our bond as we leaned on each other for support. Despite the heartache, we remained hopeful, believing that someday our prayers would be answered, and our arms would be filled with the blessings of parenthood.

But fate can be cruel, Diary. After the devastating news of my second miscarriage, followed by the doctor's grim prognosis that I can never bear children, a darkness descended upon Plato. The man I once knew, filled with boundless love and compassion, has become a stranger consumed by obsession and despair.

It pains me to see him retreat into the shadows, seeking solace in the forbidden knowledge of the occult. His once-luminous eyes now betray a haunting emptiness, as if he's glimpsed a truth too terrible to comprehend. I fear for his sanity, Diary, and for the sanctity of our love.

Yet, despite my apprehensions, I cannot abandon him in his hour of need. I will stand by his side, praying for the day when the light of love will banish the darkness that threatens to consume us both.

Until then, I shall record these troubled thoughts in the pages of this diary, a testament to the strength of our love and the hope that guides us through the darkest of nights.

Yours faithfully, Ann."

"Wow. Doesn't sound like a great marriage to me," Nancy said to no one in particular. "She wrote that over sixty-years ago."

"Skip to the back. That's usually where the juicy stuff is at," Thomas said with a smile on his face. Sullivan turns to the last entry and begins to read.

"October 31, 1959

Dear Diary,

As I pen these final words, I am overcome by a profound sense of sadness and resignation. I find myself standing on the precipice of a decision that I never imagined I would have to make. But the weight of sorrow and despair has become too much to bear, and I can no longer endure the torment that has consumed my soul.

For months now, I have watched in helpless horror as my beloved Plato has descended further into madness, consumed by his obsession with the occult and the pursuit of forbidden knowledge. He has become a mere shadow of the man I once knew, a stranger lost to the darkness that now envelops our home.

Gone are the days of laughter and love, replaced by an endless cycle of despair and isolation. Plato's once-cherished presence has become a rare occurrence, his absence marked only by the whispers of the night and the echoes of his distant footsteps.

I cannot bear to live another day in this house of shadows, haunted by the specter of a love that has long since faded into memory. My heart aches for the life we once shared, but I know now that it can never be reclaimed.

And so, with a heavy heart and tears staining my cheeks, I have made a decision that will free me from this earthly prison. I choose death over the hollow existence that awaits me within these walls, where the ghosts of our past mistakes linger like a curse upon my soul.

Let it be known that I do not seek escape out of cowardice or despair, but out of a desperate longing for peace and release. I cannot bear to watch as Plato's madness consumes us both, nor can I continue to live in the shadow of a love that has long since withered away.

And so, I bid farewell to this world of pain and sorrow, embracing the sweet oblivion that awaits me on the other side. May my sacrifice serve as a warning to those who dare to tread the path of darkness, for the price of forbidden knowledge is too high to bear.

Farewell, dear Diary, and farewell to the life that once was. May my soul find solace in the eternal embrace of oblivion, where the ghosts of our past can no longer haunt me.

Yours in sorrow and in peace, Ann

CHAPTER SIXTEEN

As Sullivan closed Ann's diary, a heavy silence descended upon the group, each member grappling with the weight of her words. Nancy glanced around the room, her eyes filled with concern as she took in the stunned expressions of her companions. Tiffany sat with tears streaming down her cheeks, her hands trembling as she clutched a worn-out handkerchief to her chest. Stu's brow furrowed in deep thought, his usually jovial demeanor replaced by a solemn expression as he processed the gravity of Ann's final decision.

Thomas, the stoic athlete, remained silent, his jaw clenched in frustration as he struggled to come to terms with the tragic fate of the Zorba family. Jeff, the stereotypical nerd, fidgeted nervously with his glasses, his usually analytical mind overwhelmed by the emotional turmoil of the moment.

Sullivan broke the silence, his voice grave as he addressed the group. "What we have just read is a testament to the darkness that lurks within these walls," he said, his tone laced with determination. "We cannot allow ourselves to be consumed by fear or despair. We must uncover the truth behind these hauntings and put an end to the suffering that has plagued this estate for far too long."

His words resonated with the group, infusing them with a renewed sense of purpose and resolve. They knew that the road ahead would be fraught with danger and uncertainty, but they were determined to face whatever challenges lay ahead.

With a shared glance and a silent nod of agreement, they rose from their seats, ready to confront the horrors that awaited them within the haunted halls of the Zorba estate. Armed with newfound courage and determination, they set out to unravel the mysteries of the past and put an end to the reign of terror that had gripped the estate for far too long.

Little did they know, their journey would lead them to confront not only the malevolent spirits that haunted the house but also the darkest depths of their own fears and insecurities. But together, they would stand united against the forces of darkness, determined to banish the ghosts of the past and bring peace to the tortured souls trapped within the walls of the Zorba estate.

As they ventured forth into the unknown, they carried with them the memory of Ann Zorba, a woman who had chosen death over despair, a tragic figure whose sacrifice would not be forgotten. And with each step they took, they vowed to honor her memory by uncovering the truth and putting an end to the cycle of suffering that had plagued the Zorba family for generations to come.

With hearts filled with determination and minds set on their mission, they pressed onward, ready to confront whatever horrors awaited them in the darkness. For they knew that only by facing their deepest fears could they hope to emerge victorious and bring an end to the haunted legacy of the Zorba estate once and for all.

As they regrouped in the grand entrance room, a chill swept down the imposing staircase. They watched in astonishment as their breath materialized in the frigid air, a tangible reminder of the unnatural cold that permeated the old estate. A piercing scream echoed from the second floor, followed by an unsettling silence broken only by the sound of a man's mournful weeping.

All eyes turned to Sullivan, silently pleading for guidance in the face of such chilling phenomena. "We must proceed to explore the upper floors," he declared, his voice steady despite the unease that gripped them all. "I would prefer Nancy and Tiffany to remain here, but it's imperative that we stick together. What I'm about to reveal is for our protection."

With measured care, Sullivan retrieved his semi-automatic from its concealed holster, eliciting a gasp of surprise from Tiffany. "I detest firearms," she confessed, her voice trembling slightly, "but under these circumstances, I'm grateful for the added security."

Their resolve steeled by Sullivan's determination and the knowledge that they were united in their quest for answers, the group braced themselves for the trials that lay ahead. Armed with both a weapon and determination, they prepared to confront the unknown horrors lurking within the shadows of the Zorba estate.

As they ascended the grand staircase to the next level of the house, their footsteps echoed ominously against the polished wood, each creak and groan of the ancient structure adding to the sense of foreboding that hung heavy in the air. Their eyes were drawn to the intricate hand-carved wooden posts and spindles, each adorned with grotesque figures of cherubic faces twisted in expressions of agony.

Reaching the top of the staircase, they found themselves faced with a daunting choice: to venture into the unknown depths of the rooms to the right or to the left. Sullivan paused, his brow furrowed in deep concentration as he tried to recall the origin of the blood-curdling scream that had pierced the silence moments before.

"I believe the scream came from this direction," he finally declared, his voice barely above a whisper as he gestured towards the right. The group exchanged wary glances, their nerves on edge as they prepared to confront whatever horrors awaited them in the darkness beyond.

Mirroring the expanse of the level below, the hallway stretched out before them, its width and length seemingly endless in the dim light. Despite the grandeur of its proportions, any sense of opulence was overshadowed by neglect and decay. A Victorian-style rug, though worn, still retained a semblance of its former glory, providing a faint glimmer of warmth against the cold, unforgiving floorboards beneath.

Yet, any illusion of grandeur was shattered by the state of the wallpaper that adorned the walls. Once resplendent with ornate patterns and rich colors, it now lay faded and discolored, its surface marred by the creeping tendrils of mold and the ravages of time. Torn and peeling in places, it whispered tales of neglect and abandonment, a silent witness to the decay that had befallen the once-proud estate.

As they made their way down the corridor, the oppressive weight of the house's history pressed down upon them, each step a reminder of the countless souls who had walked these halls before them. In the eerie stillness, the faint rustle of the wallpaper seemed to echo the mournful sighs of the past, a haunting melody that spoke of forgotten dreams and lost hopes.

"Here we are," Sullivan murmured, his voice barely above a whisper, as he adjusted his grip on the flashlight and handgun. With a sense of cautious determination, he stepped forward, his senses on high alert as he prepared to confront whatever lay beyond the threshold.

"Thomas," he called over his shoulder, his tone firm yet measured, "stand guard at the doorway. Ensure that the door remains open, no matter what."

"Consider it done, Professor," Thomas replied, his voice steady as he positioned himself directly behind Sullivan, his imposing frame a reassuring presence in the darkness.

As Sullivan tested the door and found it open, a wave of relief washed over him, tempered by the knowledge that their journey into the unknown was far from over. With Thomas at his back, he entered the room, the beams of their flashlights cutting through the gloom to reveal a scene vastly different from the decrepit corridors they had traversed thus far.

The room stretched out before them, its expansive dimensions a stark contrast to the other rooms they had inspected. The wallpaper, though faded in places, retained a semblance of its former elegance, its intricate patterns a testament to a bygone era of opulence and refinement.

At the center of the room stood a large four-poster bed, its imposing presence dominating the space with an air of regal authority. Adorned with delicate lace and plush cushions, it exuded a sense of comfort and luxury that seemed out of place amidst the decay that surrounded them.

As they took in their surroundings, Sullivan couldn't shake the feeling that they had stumbled upon something significant, something that held the key to unraveling the mysteries of the Zorba estate. With a sense of anticipation tinged with trepidation, he steeled himself for whatever revelations awaited them in the heart of the haunted room.

"The door is inching closed, Professor," Thomas exclaimed, his voice tinged with excitement as he braced himself against the stubborn resistance of the ancient wood. "But it's not too powerful... yet," he added, his muscles straining against the unseen force that threatened to seal them inside.

Outside the room, the rest of the group rallied to assist Thomas, their combined efforts barely enough to hold the door at bay against the relentless pressure that pushed against it from the other side. With every inch it closed, a palpable sense of dread filled the air, thickening the atmosphere with an oppressive weight that seemed to suffocate their very breath.

Before Sullivan could respond, he felt a chill creep over him, his breath freezing in the frigid air as tendrils of frost snaked their way across the floor. Beside him, Thomas's exhalation hung in the air like a spectral apparition, a silent testament to the unnatural cold that gripped the room.

Then, just as suddenly as it had vanished, the female scream returned, echoing through the walls with a bone-chilling intensity that sent shivers down their spines. Its eerie resonance seemed to vibrate through the very foundations of the house, a haunting reminder of the horrors that lurked within its shadowy corridors.

Upon the poster bed lay a woman draped in ethereal white, her ghostly form exuding an eerie sense of tranquility. As Sullivan approached, his footsteps muffled by heavy silence, he couldn't help but notice the spectral figure's translucent visage, her insubstantial form allowing him to see straight through her to the bedspread below.

With a sense of dread gnawing at his gut, Sullivan watched in horror as the ghostly apparition slowly opened her eyelids, revealing nothing but empty sockets where eyes should have been. A chill swept through the room as she floated effortlessly from the bed to the base, her movements devoid of the natural grace of the living.

Turning to face Sullivan with a gaze that seemed to pierce straight into his soul, the apparition spoke in a guttural voice that terrified him. "You must leave before it is too late. He knows you are here," she intoned, her words carrying the weight of centuries of anguish and despair.

As Sullivan, Thomas, and the rest of the group strained their eyes to catch a glimpse of the unfolding horror from their vantage point outside the room, they watched in stunned silence as the spectral figure produced a noose from thin air. With a cold dread settling over them like a suffocating shroud, they realized the true nature of the ghostly warning.

Without hesitation, the apparition placed the noose around her neck, the invisible force of the supernatural realm beginning to hoist her upwards with a relentless, inexorable pull. Panic-stricken, she began to gag and thrash against the invisible bonds that held her captive, her spectral form writhing in agony as she fought against the inevitable.

Then, in a horrifying spectacle that seared itself into the minds of all who witnessed it, the rope tightened around her neck, cutting off her ghostly cries as her form dissolved into wisps of vapor, vanishing before their eyes in a chilling reminder of the perilous fate that awaited those who dared to linger too long in the haunted depths of the Zorba estate.

CHAPTER SEVENTEEN

SILENCE ENVELOPED THE room as the door yielded to Thomas's strength, granting entrance to the group. With cautious steps, they crossed the threshold into the chamber, their hearts heavy with trepidation. Sullivan, the weight of responsibility heavy upon his shoulders, moved with purpose, his gaze sweeping over the room in search of answers.

Without explanation, he approached the largest dresser, its ornate mirror casting warped reflections of their anxious faces. In a gesture that seemed almost involuntary, Sullivan placed Ann's diary upon its polished surface, the heavy thud of its weight echoing in the hushed room.

All eyes were drawn to the diary as if sensing its significance, anticipation crackling in the air like static electricity. In the eerie stillness, the haunting scream of the woman pierced the silence once more, sending a shiver down their spines.

Then, as if summoned by the spectral call, the ghostly apparition materialized before them, its ethereal form hovering over the dresser with an otherworldly grace. With a sense of solemn purpose, it reached for a pen, its movements fluid and precise as it turned the diary to its final pages.

Sullivan watched in awe as the ghostly figure began to write, its penmanship as delicate and elegant as if etched by an angel's hand. Words flowed effortlessly onto the page, each stroke imbued with a weight of centuries-old wisdom and sorrow. Ignoring the group's presence, the apparition continued to inscribe its message, a silent witness to the unfolding events.

Minutes stretched into eternity as the figure wrote, its form flickering like a candle in the wind. And then, with a final flourish, it vanished into the ether, leaving behind nothing but a lingering sense of foreboding in its wake.

With trembling hands, Sullivan turned the diary around to read the words that had been left behind, knowing that they held the key to unlocking the secrets of the haunted estate and the tragic fate of those who had come before them.

"As I pen these words, I do so with a heavy heart and a soul weighed down by the burden of unspeakable horrors. I pray that you all may find the strength to heed my warning and escape the clutches of the darkness that threatens to consume you."

"Before I took my own life, I learned the truth about my late husband, Plato Zorba, and the atrocities he

committed within the walls of our once-beloved home. No longer content with his futile search for ghosts, he turned to far more sinister pursuits, abandoning his humanity in pursuit of power and control."

"Plato's obsession with the supernatural drove him to unspeakable acts of cruelty. No longer satisfied with the spirits that haunted our estate, he began to kidnap innocent children and young adults, their lives sacrificed upon the altar of his twisted desires."

"I cannot bear to recount the horrors that unfolded within these walls, the screams of the innocent echoing in my mind like a never-ending nightmare. My beloved husband, once a man of intellect and charm, became a monster consumed by madness, his soul tainted by the darkness that lurked within him."

"But even in death, Plato's malevolent spirit continues to haunt this house, his victims trapped within its walls, their restless souls crying out for release. It is only by freeing them from their torment that we may hope to escape the curse that binds us to this place."

"My dear reader, I implore you to heed my words and take heed of the path that lies before you. The only way to escape the clutches of this house and the darkness that dwells within is to free the souls of its inhabitants, to release them from their eternal torment and bring an end to the reign of terror that has plagued us for far too long."

"It will not be easy. He will kill every one of you if you do not escape. May you find the courage to confront the

horrors that await you within these walls, and may you emerge victorious in the face of unspeakable evil.

With deepest regret and remorse,

Ann Zorba

The doors to the rooms on the floor began to creak open, their hinges groaning in protest as unseen forces slammed them shut with a resounding thud. The sound of a male voice, distorted by pain and rage, echoed through the corridors, growing louder with each passing moment as it drew nearer to their location. It was as if the very walls of the estate were rebelling against the shocking revelations that had been unearthed.

A fierce wind tore through the halls, whipping at their clothes and hair with an otherworldly force, as if intent on driving them back from the truth that lay hidden within the haunted walls. Sensing the imminent danger, Sullivan wasted no time in issuing his command, his voice strained with urgency. "Quick, we need to get back downstairs," he ordered, his gaze darting nervously into the darkness as he trailed behind the group, his weapon poised and ready to confront whatever malevolent force lurked in the shadows.

But as they hurried back towards the safety of the grand entry hall, fate had other plans in store for them.

Instead of emerging into the familiar surroundings of the main foyer, they found themselves standing amidst the towering shelves of the library, the heavy wooden door clicking shut behind them with a finality that sent a shiver down their spines.

"How did we end up here?" a terrified Tiffany asked. "I was sure we were going in the right direction.

Sullivan wasted no time in securing the door, his hands trembling slightly as he slid the heavy bolt into place. The groans and curses that had plagued them on the upper floor seemed to have subsided, their eerie echoes fading into the oppressive silence of the library.

As they took in their surroundings, Sullivan's gaze fell upon the roaring fire that blazed merrily in the hearth, its flickering flames casting dancing shadows across the room. "Who started the fire?" he demanded, his voice tinged with suspicion as he turned to face the group.

Their faces mirrored his own confusion, each one shaking their head in bewilderment as they struggled to comprehend the surreal events that had unfolded before them. Thomas, the stalwart athlete, spoke up first, his voice tinged with disbelief. "Sorry, Doc," he muttered, "but this is getting crazy. Two ghosts, hidden rooms, and now a ghost that actually wrote to us? It's like something out of a nightmare."

With a heavy silence descending upon the room, they knew that they were facing a threat far greater than they had ever imagined. But as they huddled together in the flickering light of the fire, they also knew that they could not afford to back down, not when the truth lay tantalizingly within their grasp, waiting to be uncovered in the depths of the haunted Zorba estate.

CHAPTER EIGHTEEN

AS THE GROUP gathered in the safety of the library, the flickering flames of the fire casting a warm glow against the walls, Sullivan's voice broke the heavy silence that hung over them like a shroud. "I think our best course of action now is to try and make our way back to the kitchen," he suggested, his tone calm but resolute. "It's a central location where we can regroup, brainstorm our next steps, and perhaps get something to eat to bolster our spirits."

As they nodded in agreement, Sullivan took a moment to recount a tale that he believed shed light on their current predicament. "Have any of you heard of the Winchester Mystery House in San Jose, California?" he asked, his eyes searching their faces for recognition. "Legend has it that Sarah Winchester, the heiress to the Winchester fortune, consulted with a spiritualist who told her that she could attain immortality if she continued to build onto her already massive home."

He paused, allowing the weight of his words to sink in before continuing. "Sarah Winchester believed that by constantly expanding her house, she could confuse and evade the spirits of those killed by Winchester rifles, seeking to appease their restless souls and avoid their wrath."

Sullivan's gaze swept over the group, his expression grave as he drew parallels between Sarah Winchester's folly and the madness that had consumed Plato Zorba. "I can't help but feel that Plato Zorba may have been driven by a similar delusion," he confessed, his voice tinged with sorrow. "Perhaps in his madness, he believed that by continuously adding onto this estate, he could escape the ghosts of his past and achieve some form of immortality."

He gestured towards the intricately carved shelves that lined the walls of the library, their contents a testament to the labyrinthine nature of the Zorba estate. "This place is like a massive puzzle," he mused, his eyes scanning the room with a mixture of fascination and apprehension. "It's easy to get lost in its depths, to lose yourself in the endless corridors and hidden passages that seem to stretch on forever."

With a shared sense of determination, the group rose to their feet, ready to confront the challenges that lay ahead. Armed with Sullivan's insight and fueled by the flickering flames of the fire, they set out once more into the darkness, their resolve unshaken even in the face of the unknown horrors that awaited them in the haunted halls of the Zorba estate.

As the group navigated the labyrinthine corridors of the Zorba estate, they exchanged observations and insights, each member contributing their thoughts in an effort to find their way back to the kitchen. "This situation reminds me of the Stephen King movie, Rose Red," Jeff remarked, his voice tinged with a hint of unease. "In the movie, they used rope to retrace their steps and find their way out."

Nancy nodded in agreement, a wistful tone coloring her words as she spoke. "Having something like that would certainly make things easier right about now," she replied, her gaze scanning the dimly lit hallway with a mixture of apprehension and determination.

As they continued their journey through the twisting corridors of the estate, the echoes of their footsteps mingling with the oppressive silence that surrounded them, they couldn't shake the feeling that they were being watched, that unseen eyes followed their every move with a malevolent intent.

Finally, they found the kitchen. Nancy suggested that she make a pot of coffee for everyone. Tiffany joined her. Small talk broke out between Jeff, Thomas and Stu as Sullivan decided to read Ann Zorba's diary from beginning to end.

After Sullivan finishes reading Ann Zorba's diary, he clears his throat, the weight of the revelations heavy on his mind. The group gathers around, their faces expectant yet apprehensive. With a somber tone, Sullivan begins to recount the disturbing account of Dr. Plato Zorba's descent into madness.

"As I delved into Ann's diary," Sullivan begins, "I uncovered the harrowing truth about Dr. Zorba's obsession with the supernatural. Following notification that Ann could not have children, he began his travels across the globe, collecting ghosts to populate his macabre collection within these walls and descended further into darkness.

Not content with merely trapping spirits, he turned to kidnapping children and young adults, subjecting them to unspeakable torture and ultimately condemning them to a fate worse than death, forever trapped within these cursed confines."

The group listens in horrified silence as Sullivan continues, his voice trembling slightly with the weight of the atrocities he describes. "What's most chilling," he adds, "is the references to a lower level within the estate, where the most heinous acts took place. It seems that this house holds secrets far more sinister than we could have ever imagined."

"I told you that I thought there was more to the story about this house," Tiffany added.

Sullivan pauses, his gaze lingering on the group before continuing, "Ann's diary contains numerous references to a level below where we currently stand. It seems that this underground chamber was the heart of Dr. Zorba's atrocities, where the innocent were subjected to unimaginable torment before meeting their tragic ends."

He gestures towards the floor, his expression grave. "It is there, in the depths of this house, that the true horrors of Zorba's madness lie. The very thought of what transpired in those dark corridors is enough to chill the blood."

Nancy shudders, her eyes wide with fear, while Tiffany clutches onto Stu's arm, seeking comfort in his presence. Even Thomas, the stoic athlete, looks visibly unsettled by Sullivan's words.

"But we cannot let fear paralyze us," Sullivan continues, his voice resolute. "We must confront the darkness head-on, for it is only by unraveling the secrets of this house that we stand any chance of freeing the trapped souls and putting an end to this nightmare and freeing us from the confides of the house."

As the group gathered in the kitchen, sipping on their steaming cups of coffee and nibbling on the snacks Tiffany had laid out, Sullivan's mind was already at work, devising a plan to uncover the passage to the basement. The weight of Ann Zorba's revelations pressed heavily upon him, fueling his determination to confront the darkest depths of the estate.

With each sip of coffee, Sullivan mulled over the information gleaned from Ann's diary, piecing together clues like shards of a fractured puzzle. He knew that the key to unlocking the secrets of the house lay in finding the hidden entrance to the lower level, where the horrors of Dr. Zorba's madness were said to have unfolded.

As the aroma of freshly brewed coffee filled the air, Sullivan glanced around the kitchen, his gaze lingering on each member of the group in turn. They were his allies in this perilous endeavor, each with their own strengths and skills to contribute to the search.

Nancy, with her sharp intellect and keen eye for detail, would be invaluable in uncovering hidden clues. Stu, with his steady resolve and unwavering courage, would provide the backbone of support needed to face whatever horrors awaited them below. Tiffany's intuitive nature and connection to the spiritual realm could prove instrumental in navigating the ethereal labyrinth of the house.

And then there was Thomas, the stalwart athlete whose physical prowess would be essential in overcoming any obstacles they might encounter along the way. Finally, Jeff, the stereotypical nerd, whose knowledge of technology and gadgetry could provide a technological edge in their exploration.

With his plan taking shape in his mind, Sullivan set down his coffee cup and addressed the group, his voice steady despite the gravity of their task. "We need to find the entrance to the basement," he began, his words carrying a sense of urgency. "According to Ann's diary, that's where the heart of the darkness lies. If we're going to have any hope of freeing the trapped souls and putting an end to this nightmare, we need to start there."

The group nodded in agreement, their resolve firm as they prepared to embark on the next phase of their journey. With their cups of coffee drained and their snacks forgotten, they rose from the kitchen table, ready to confront the unknown and delve into the shadowed depths of the haunted estate.

CHAPTER NINETEEN

SULLIVAN'S DIRECTIVE CUT through the tension in the room, his voice carrying a sense of purpose that spurred the group into action. "I'd like us all to convene in the grand entrance hallway," he instructed, his tone firm yet measured. "We'll need to utilize some of our equipment for the search of the lower level. It's imperative that we stick together throughout the process."

Tiffany's response elicited a ripple of laughter from the group, her light-hearted remark momentarily easing the weight of their grim task. "You can count on that," she quipped, a playful glint in her eye as she exchanged knowing looks with her companions.

As they made their way towards the grand entrance hallway, the group moved with a newfound sense of purpose, their footsteps echoing against the polished marble floors. Sullivan led the way, his mind already racing with plans and strategies for the search ahead.

Upon reaching the grand entrance, Sullivan motioned for the group to gather around, their faces illuminated by lights Jeff and Stu had set up. With practiced efficiency, he began distributing the equipment they would need for their exploration: flashlights, EMF meters, and other tools designed to detect paranormal activity.

"This equipment will be our eyes and ears in the darkness," Sullivan explained, his voice tinged with a sense of gravitas. "But remember, our greatest strength lies in our unity. We must remain vigilant and support one another every step of the way."

With a solemn nod of agreement, the group prepared to descend into the depths of the house, their resolve unwavering in the face of the unknown. Together, they would confront the darkness that lurked within the shadows, determined to uncover the truth and put an end to the torment that plagued the haunted estate.

"Thomas," Sullivan began, his voice commanding yet tinged with a hint of urgency, "I need you to set up a motion detector as a kind of trap. Position it strategically so that we can monitor any movement behind us while we focus on locating the entrance to the lower level. Use your expertise to aim it towards key areas: the entrance, the kitchen, and here in the grand entrance."

Thomas nodded, his expression serious as he accepted the task at hand. "Consider it done, Professor," he replied, his tone determined as he began to assess the best placement for the motion detector.

Turning to Nancy, Sullivan continued, his gaze shifting to the young woman beside him. “Nancy, I want you to carry the temperature recorder,” he instructed, handing her the device. “It will alert us to any sudden changes in temperature, much like the ones we’ve already experienced. A drop in temperature could signal the imminent manifestation of an apparition.”

Nancy nodded in understanding, clutching the recorder tightly in her hand as she prepared to fulfill her role in the exploration.

“What would you like for me to do Professor?” Tiffany asked.

Tiffany’s question drew Sullivan’s attention next, prompting him to hand her a pair of special viewing glasses with a hopeful expression. “Tiffany,” he said, his voice softening slightly, “I’m entrusting you with these. They haven’t worked for me, but perhaps your intuition and sensitivity to the occult, as demonstrated by your experience with the blood on the door frame, will allow you to see something that eludes the rest of us.”

Tiffany accepted the glasses with a nod, her eyes shining with determination as she slipped them on, eager to lend her unique abilities to the group’s efforts.

As Sullivan turned to address Stu and Jeff, he gestured towards the recording equipment they carried. “Stu, Jeff, your task is crucial,” he stated, his voice carrying a note of gravity. “Record everything.

If a ghost decides to make an appearance, I want you two to capture it on film."

Stu and Jeff exchanged a glance, their expressions a mix of excitement and apprehension as they prepared to document whatever phenomena awaited them.

With each member of the group assigned their role, Sullivan reached for his gun, a symbol of his commitment to their safety. "And as for me," he declared, the nervous laughter that followed punctuating his words, "I'll provide security."

As the laughter subsided and silence fell over the room, Sullivan glanced around at his team, a sense of determination burning in his eyes. "Is everyone ready?" he asked, his voice steady and sure.

One by one, the group nodded in affirmation, their resolve unwavering as they prepared to embark on their mission into the unknown. With each member poised to fulfill their role, they stood united against the darkness that awaited them, ready to confront whatever horrors lay hidden within the depths of the haunted estate.

With Thomas's confirmation that the motion detector system had been successfully set up, Sullivan wasted no time in addressing the group, his gaze sweeping over each member with a sense of purpose. "Ann's diary unfortunately didn't provide us with the exact location of the entrance to the lower level," he began, his voice steady despite the uncertainty of their task. "But I believe Dr. Zorba intentionally obscured its whereabouts, likely concealing it within one of the many hidden rooms scattered throughout his mansion."

He paused, his brow furrowing in concentration as he considered their next course of action. "Given that Ann's bedroom is situated almost directly above us," Sullivan continued, "I doubt that Zorba would have placed the entrance to his torture chamber in such close proximity. Therefore, I propose that we concentrate our search on the rear rooms of this floor."

As the group absorbed his words, Sullivan withdrew several markers from his jacket pocket, each one a tangible reminder of their commitment to the task at hand. "Much like Hansel and Gretel leaving breadcrumbs," he explained, handing out the markers to each member, "we'll use these markers to guide our way back to this point. I'll lead the group, and don't worry if you mark a wall at the same time as someone else. It'll make it easier for us to spot our trail on the return journey."

With the markers distributed and their plan in place, Sullivan motioned for the group to follow him as they set off towards the rear rooms of the mansion. Each step forward was a step deeper into the unknown, but with their markers to guide them and their resolve unyielding, they were ready to face whatever trials lay ahead. Together, they moved forward, united in their quest to uncover the secrets hidden within the haunted estate and bring an end to the torment that plagued its halls.

"I hate these hallways," Tiffany confessed, her voice carrying a hint of unease as she glanced around at the oppressive walls closing in on them. "When I was a teenager, my grandfather took our whole family to Vietnam. He did two tours of duty there in the 1960s and wanted to see it one more time before he passed away a year later. He said he wanted to pay his respects to the friends he lost in the jungle."

"Why not just visit the Vietnam War wall they have in D.C.?" Jeff interjected, curiosity evident in his tone.

"We suggested that," Tiffany replied, her gaze distant as she recalled the memories of that trip. "But he was adamant that we travel with him so that the next generations would never forget what happened there. One of the places we visited was the tunnels of Cu Chi."

"What are those?" Nancy inquired, her interest piqued.

"They were a series of underground tunnels built by the Vietnamese," Tiffany explained, turning to Sullivan for assistance. "Professor, perhaps you could explain it better than I can."

Sullivan nodded, seizing the opportunity to divert their attention from the ominous hallway. "Before the Americans arrived in Vietnam, the Vietnamese were fighting for their independence from France," he began, his voice steady as he launched into the history lesson. "Realizing that they were outmatched in terms of firepower, they dug these tunnels, stretching over 150 miles. From there, they could move undetected and launch surprise attacks on the invading forces."

"I've seen the tunnels myself, and they're quite impressive," Sullivan continued, his gaze thoughtful as he recalled his own experiences. "Underground, it was cooler in the summer, and the Vietcong could emerge from trapdoors, strike swiftly, and then vanish just as quickly. They had booby traps set up that made it incredibly dangerous for anyone foolish enough to enter."

"I agree, Tiffany," Sullivan concluded, turning back to her with a reassuring smile. "These halls do have a similar claustrophobic feel to them, seemingly stretching on for miles. But we'll press on together, just like the soldiers who navigated those tunnels in Vietnam."

CHAPTER TWENTY

DOOR AFTER DOOR. Room after room. No access to a sub-level was found. Sullivan could sense that not only frustration but depression was setting in. "Let's take a break, everyone," he suggested, his voice tinged with urgency. "I know we're all tired, but we must find a way out of this house."

As the group paused to catch their breath, a sudden roar shattered the stillness, echoing through the corridors with an otherworldly intensity. The sound of a bullwhip crackling through the air sent shockwaves rippling through the group, eliciting screams of terror from Nancy and Tiffany.

Instinctively, they ran towards Sullivan, seeking refuge in his presence as he stood at the forefront, his gun raised and pointed down the hallway from where the sounds had emanated. His expression was tense, his senses on high alert as he scanned the shadows for any sign of danger.

In the midst of the chaos, the ghostly apparition of the lion tamer materialized before them, accompanied by the spectral form of his lion. The sight sent a chill down Sullivan's spine, but he stood his ground, his resolve unyielding in the face of the supernatural.

With a silent gesture, the lion tamer directed their attention towards a door further down the hallway, his message clear even without words. Sullivan exchanged a determined glance with his companions, their fear momentarily eclipsed by a shared sense of purpose.

"We need to keep moving," Sullivan declared, his voice steady despite the lingering unease that gripped them all like icy tendrils. "Whatever lies beyond that door, we'll face it together."

With a sense of foreboding hanging heavy in the air, Sullivan approached the door, his hand trembling slightly as he reached out to grasp the handle. But when he tried the door, unlike the others they had encountered, he found it locked, stubbornly resisting their efforts to gain entry.

"Okay, big guy, this is where you come in," Sullivan said, turning to Thomas with a forced smile, though his heart raced with apprehension. Thomas, with his towering frame and strength, seemed their best hope to overcome the obstacle before them.

With a determined nod, Thomas stepped forward, his muscles tensing in anticipation of the task ahead. His first attempt to break the door free met with resistance, the sturdy lock holding firm against his efforts. Frustration flickered across his face, quickly giving way to determination as he withdrew from the door, positioning himself a few feet back.

With a primal roar, Thomas threw his shoulder and weight into the door with all his might. The sound of splintering wood filled the air as the door lock shattered, the barrier giving way with a violent crash. As the door flung open, a hissing sound emanated from within, sending a shiver down the group's collective spine.

The darkness beyond the threshold seemed to swallow them whole, a tangible sense of dread hanging heavy in the air. With cautious steps, Sullivan led the way into the room, his senses on high alert for any sign of danger lurking in the shadows.

As they ventured further into the unknown, the oppressive atmosphere seemed to close in around them, suffocating in its intensity. Every creak of the floorboards, every whisper of movement, sent a jolt of fear coursing through their veins, their nerves stretched taut with anticipation of what horrors awaited them in the depths of the haunted mansion.

The room lay shrouded in darkness, illuminated only by the feeble beams of everyone's flashlights. But despite their efforts to pierce the gloom, the space appeared barren, devoid of any furnishings or adornments save for the peeling wallpaper that clung desperately to the walls like faded memories of a bygone era.

Sullivan could sense the frustration mounting within the group, a palpable tension that hung heavy in the stagnant air. With a quick glance around the room, he knew they needed to find a way forward, a glimmer of hope to cling to in the face of the encroaching darkness.

"Let's try pounding on the walls," Sullivan suggested, his voice cutting through the silence with a sense of urgency. "Maybe if we make enough noise, we'll attract some attention."

Tiffany and Nancy hesitated for a moment but with a shared nod of determination, they stepped forward to join in the effort. Their fists pounded against the walls in a rhythmic cadence, the sound echoing through the empty room like a desperate plea for salvation.

But then, just as quickly as they had begun, they froze in place, their eyes widening in disbelief as the room began to fill with a soft, ethereal light. The air was filled with the haunting strains of carnival music, a discordant melody.

The unmistakable roar of a lion and the crack of a bullwhip reverberated through the room, causing Sullivan and the others to exchange uneasy glances. And then, from a wall they had not yet touched, a figure began to materialize, its form flickering in and out of existence like a ghostly apparition. They could not bring the image into focus.

Tiffany raised the special glasses. She screamed. "It's the lion tamer again," she shouted. The lion tamer, partly emerging from the wall as if beckoning them to enter. With a wave of its spectral hand, it seemed to invite the group forward, a silent invitation to discover what secrets lay beyond the threshold. "He wants us to follow him," Tiffany said a little less nervous than before.

Sullivan's heart pounded in his chest as he exchanged a wary glance with his companions. Whatever lay beyond that wall, he knew they had no choice but to press forward, to confront the darkness head-on in their quest for answers. With a steadying breath, he stepped forward, leading the way into the unknown, his resolve unwavering despite the growing sense of unease that gnawed at his soul.

As the group cautiously approached the wall that the lion tamer had seemingly emerged from, they sense trepidation. Their flashlights cast flickering shadows that danced across the peeling wallpaper, lending an eerie quality to the dimly lit room. With trembling hands, Sullivan reached out to touch the wall, his fingers tracing the faded outline of what appeared to be a hidden panel.

With a hesitant push, the panel slid aside with a soft, ominous creak, revealing a narrow staircase that descended into darkness below. The air grew colder, a chill creeping up their spines as they exchanged uneasy glances. There was no turning back now; they were committed to uncovering the secrets that lay hidden within the depths of the mansion.

With cautious steps, Sullivan led the way down the staircase, the others following close behind, their footsteps muffled by the oppressive silence that enveloped them. The air grew thick with the scent of decay, the musty odor of ancient secrets long forgotten.

As they reached the bottom of the stairs, their flashlights revealed a sight that sent a shiver down their spines. Before them lay a torture chamber straight out of their darkest nightmares, its walls lined with sinister-looking instruments of torture used during the Spanish Inquisition.

Iron maidens stood like silent sentinels, their spiked interiors gleaming ominously in the dim light. Stretching racks creaked with the weight of unseen victims, while devices designed to inflict unimaginable pain loomed ominously in the shadows.

The air was heavy with the echoes of suffering long past, whispers of anguish that seemed to linger in the air like a malevolent presence. Sullivan and his companions exchanged horrified looks, their hearts pounding in their chests as they realized the true nature of the chamber they had stumbled upon.

With a sense of dread gnawing at their souls, they knew that they had stumbled upon something far more sinister than they could have ever imagined. As they stood in the depths of the torture chamber, surrounded by the echoes of centuries-old horrors, they knew that they were in for a nightmarish journey into the darkest depths of human depravity.

As the group cautiously approached the wall that the lion tamer had seemingly emerged from, a sense of trepidation hung heavy in the air. Their flashlights cast flickering shadows that danced across the peeling wallpaper, lending an eerie quality to the dimly lit room. With trembling hands, Sullivan reached out to touch the wall, his fingers tracing the faded outline of what appeared to be a hidden panel.

Sullivan's mind raced with a mixture of fear and curiosity. What secrets lay hidden beyond this mysterious wall? Could they be on the verge of uncovering the truth behind the mansion's haunting?

Tiffany's pulse quickened as she stared into the yawning darkness of the staircase. A sense of foreboding gripped her heart, but she knew they had come too far to turn back now. With a deep breath, she steeled herself for whatever horrors awaited them below.

Thomas felt a knot form in the pit of his stomach as he descended the stairs, his mind flashing with images of the torture chamber that lay in wait. The thought of what they might find filled him with a sense of dread, but he knew he had to stay strong for the sake of the group.

Nancy's thoughts were a jumble of fear and fascination as she followed behind the others. The prospect of discovering the secrets hidden within the mansion both thrilled and terrified her in equal measure. What dark truths awaited them in the depths below?

As they reached the bottom of the stairs, their flashlights revealed a sight that sent a shiver down their spines. Before them lay a torture chamber straight out of their darkest nightmares, its walls lined with sinister-looking instruments of torture used during the Spanish Inquisition.

The air was heavy with the echoes of suffering long past, whispers of anguish that seemed to linger in the air like a malevolent presence. Nancy's breath caught in her throat as she took in the scene before her, her mind reeling with horror at the thought of the atrocities that had been committed within these walls.

But amidst the darkness and despair, a glimmer of hope emerged. Nancy's flashlight caught sight of something lying on one of the torture tables: a large dust-covered journal, its pages yellowed with age. With trembling hands, she reached out and picked it up, her heart pounding in her chest as she realized what she held in her hands.

It was the journal of Dr. Plato Zorba, the man responsible for the horrors that had unfolded within these walls. As Nancy flipped through its pages, her stomach churned with a mixture of revulsion and fascination. Here, in her hands, lay the key to unlocking the mysteries of the haunted estate and uncovering the truth behind its dark past.

CHAPTER TWENTY-ONE

"PROFESSOR," NANCY'S VOICE quivered with fear, her words cutting through the oppressive silence like a knife. "The temperature is starting to drop quickly."

Sullivan's blood ran cold as he turned to face her, his heart hammering in his chest with a mounting sense of dread. The air seemed to grow thick with an icy chill, a tangible manifestation of the terror that gripped them all.

Turning to Stu and Jeff, Sullivan's voice was strained with urgency. "Did you record this whole room?" he asked, his tone edged with desperation.

"Yes," they both replied in unison, their voices tinged with unease. "I think we even have the lion tamer coming out and in the wall," Jeff added, his words sending a shiver down their spines.

Sullivan's grip tightened on his flashlight, his mind racing with a desperate need to escape the horrors that surrounded them. "Great," he muttered, his voice barely above a whisper. "I think it would be a good idea to get out of here."

As Sullivan led the group back up the staircase, a sense of impending doom hung heavy in the air, suffocating in its intensity. But just as they thought they were safe, a gut-wrenching groan echoed through the room, vibrating the very walls around them.

Thomas, the last person on the stairs, froze in terror as he heard the sound, his heart pounding in his chest like a drumbeat of doom. Slowly, he turned, only to come face to face with a ghastly apparition emerging from the walls before him.

Even without the aid of the special glasses, Thomas could see the twisted visage of Dr. Plato Zorba, his spectral form reaching out with claw-like hands, intent on dragging him into the depths of despair.

With a primal scream, Thomas fought back with all his strength, kicking and thrashing as he struggled to break free from Zorba's grasp. With a final surge of adrenaline, he reached the safety of the floor above, slamming the door shut behind him with a deafening crash. He placed his body against the door, but realized it was only a temporary solution.

But the nightmare was far from over. The ghostly pounding and groaning persisted, each blow reverberating through the walls like a relentless drumbeat of death. With a sense of desperation, Sullivan barked orders to Stu and Jeff, their hands trembling as they searched for something, anything, to hold back the encroaching darkness.

Finally, they returned with a steady wooden chair, its sturdy frame offering a glimmer of hope in the face of overwhelming terror. With trembling hands, Sullivan inserted it under the broken door handle, the makeshift brace holding back the relentless onslaught of the vengeful spirit.

For agonizing moments that stretched into eternity, they waited, their breaths held in fearful anticipation. And then, mercifully, the pounding and groaning ceased, leaving them in a suffocating silence broken only by the ragged gasps of their own terrified breaths.

But as they huddled together in the darkness, they knew that their ordeal was far from over. The haunted mansion held more horrors than they could ever imagine, and they were trapped in its grasp, prisoners to the malevolent forces that lurked within its shadowy depths.

"Professor, you can have this," Nancy said, handing Zorba's journal to Sullivan.

"Alright, everyone, let's follow the marking on the wall and regroup in the grand entrance hall," Professor Sullivan announced, his voice betraying a hint of urgency. "We need to delve into Zorba's journal. Perhaps within its pages, we'll uncover clues that could lead us out of this nightmare and provide solace for the tormented spirits trapped within these walls."

With a mixture of apprehension and determination, the group followed Sullivan's lead, retracing their steps through the labyrinthine corridors of the mansion. Each footfall echoed ominously against the cold stone floors, a stark reminder of the mansion's dark history and the malevolent forces that lurked within.

As they entered the grand entrance hall, the group gathered around Sullivan, bracing themselves for what revelations the journal might hold. With trembling hands, Sullivan opened the journal and began to read aloud, the words on the yellowed pages painting a macabre portrait of Zorba's descent into madness and the atrocities he had committed within these very walls.

As Sullivan's voice resonated through the hall, a cacophony of chaos erupted from the nearby kitchen, shattering the uneasy calm that had settled over the mansion. The metallic clang of pots and pans reverberated off the stone walls, mingling with the spine-chilling echo of a bloodcurdling scream that pierced the air like a dagger. A cold shiver raced down their spines as they exchanged nervous glances, their hearts pounding in their chests.

"Tiffany, bring the glasses!" Sullivan's command sliced through the tension, snapping them into action as they hurried towards the kitchen, their footsteps echoing loudly in the empty corridor. With each step closer to the source of the disturbance, their apprehension grew, tendrils of fear wrapping around their hearts like icy tendrils.

Arriving at the entrance of the kitchen, they were greeted by a scene straight out of a nightmare. Pots and pans flew through the air in a chaotic frenzy, propelled by an unseen force. Amidst the chaos, an angry male voice shouted in Italian, his words dripping with venom, while a woman's terrified screams pierced the tumultuous air.

The ghostly apparitions within the kitchen remained elusive, their forms flickering in and out of focus like ethereal shadows. But Tiffany, with an eerie clarity that sent shivers down their spines, stepped forward, her gaze locked on the ghastly spectacle unfolding before them.

"Oh my God," she gasped, her voice trembling with horror. "It's one of the 13 ghosts you talk about, Professor. It's the chef, and he's chasing his wife around the kitchen, wielding a meat cleaver like a deranged madman."

As Tiffany handed the glasses to Sullivan, her complexion turned ashen, her hands trembling with shock. "I-I can't look anymore," she stammered, retreating to the safety of the group, her eyes unable to bear witness to the grisly scene unfolding before them.

With a sense of grim determination, Sullivan donned the glasses, the lenses revealing a nightmare realm hidden from mortal eyes. The spectral form of the chef materialized before him, his visage twisted in rage as he brandished the blood-stained cleaver, his wife's terrified form darting desperately around the kitchen like a frightened doe.

A sickening sensation churned in Sullivan's stomach as he watched in horror, powerless to intervene as the gruesome tableau unfolded before him. "Yes, Tiffany, this is Emilio, the chef that supposedly killed his mother-in-law and wife." The air was thick with the metallic tang of blood, mingling with the pungent aroma of fear and despair.

With a final, gut-wrenching scream, the woman collided with the wall, her form dissolving into wisps of ectoplasmic mist before vanishing from sight. But the chef, consumed by madness and driven by an insatiable thirst for vengeance, pursued her relentlessly into the unknown depths of the mansion, his spectral form fading into the darkness like a ghostly specter.

With a heavy sigh of relief, Sullivan removed the glasses, his eyes blinking rapidly to adjust to the sudden clarity of the kitchen. "It's all clear," he declared, his voice tinged with a mixture of exhaustion and grim resolve. "The apparitions are gone."

Surveying the aftermath of the spectral chaos, Sullivan's gaze swept over the disarrayed kitchen, taking in the scattered debris and the lingering traces of otherworldly disturbances. Pots and pans lay strewn across the floor like discarded playthings, a testament to the violent frenzy that had unfolded moments before.

"Ladies," Sullivan addressed the group with a gentle but authoritative tone, "if you don't mind, perhaps you can locate the Tupperware with our food items and salvage what you can." Despite the lingering tension in the air, he maintained a sense of composure, his leadership unwavering even in the face of supernatural adversity.

Turning to his companions, Sullivan swiftly formulated a plan of action to regroup and assess their situation. “Stu, Jeff,” he addressed the two men with a nod, “stay with the ladies and assist them in gathering our supplies.” He trusted in their abilities to provide support and reassurance to the group, their presence a stabilizing force amidst the chaos.

“Thomas,” Sullivan turned to his remaining companion, his expression serious, “you and I will return to the grand entrance. I want to check the recordings on our instruments.” There was a sense of urgency in his voice, a determination to uncover any clues that might shed light on the mysteries of the mansion and its spectral inhabitants.

With their roles assigned and their objectives clear, the group sprang into action, each member rallying to fulfill their assigned tasks. As they navigated the eerie corridors of the mansion, Sullivan’s mind raced with questions and uncertainties, his resolve unwavering in the face of the unknown. For within the heart of darkness, the key to their salvation awaited, hidden amidst the secrets and shadows that lurked within.

CHAPTER TWENTY-TWO

As Sullivan and Thomas made their way back to the grand entrance, their footsteps echoed softly against the cold stone floors, the eerie silence of the mansion enveloping them like a suffocating shroud. With each passing moment, the weight of the supernatural phenomena they had witnessed pressed down upon them, a tangible reminder of the malevolent forces that lurked within.

Arriving at their destination, Sullivan wasted no time in retrieving the instruments they had brought with them, his hands trembling slightly with anticipation as he powered up the motion detector and temperature readouts. As the devices hummed to life, a sense of apprehension hung heavy in the air, their flickering screens serving as windows into the unseen realm of the supernatural.

Glancing at the motion detector's display, Sullivan's heart sank as he observed numerous blips of movement scattered across the screen, each one indicating the presence of spectral entities traversing the mansion's corridors. The realization sent a chill down his spine, the magnitude of their situation weighing heavily upon him as he grappled with the implications of their findings.

But it was the temperature readouts that truly astounded them, the data painting a vivid picture of the spectral energies that permeated the mansion's walls. As Sullivan studied the readings, his eyes widening in disbelief, he noted a significant drop in temperature corresponding to the areas where the apparitions had been sighted. It was as if the very presence of the spirits had sapped the warmth from the air, leaving behind an icy chill that seeped into their bones.

"Remarkable," Sullivan murmured, his voice barely above a whisper as he processed the implications of their discoveries. "The temperature fluctuations correspond perfectly to the presence of the spirits. It's as if their very essence is altering the fabric of reality itself."

Thomas nodded in agreement, his expression a mixture of awe and trepidation as he studied the readouts alongside Sullivan. The significance of their findings was not lost on either of them, the data serving as a testament to the sheer power and malevolence of the entities that inhabited the mansion.

As they continued to analyze the data, a sense of urgency gripped them, their quest for answers propelled forward by the chilling truths they had uncovered. For within the depths of the grand entrance hall, amidst the flickering lights and humming machinery, lay the key to unlocking the mysteries of the haunted estate and the horrors that lay within.

"Let's head back to the kitchen," Sullivan said. "Just leave the equipment here."

In the dimly lit kitchen of the sprawling Zorba estate, the group gathered around the table, their hunger pangs momentarily forgotten as they eagerly awaited Sullivan's next move. With the weight of Dr. Plato Zorba's journal in his hands, Sullivan's fingers traced the weathered leather cover, a tangible link to the secrets hidden within its pages.

As the others began to partake in the modest meal they had salvaged from the chaos of the kitchen, Sullivan delved into the journal, his eyes scanning the handwritten entries with a mixture of curiosity and trepidation. The first entry he came across spoke of Zorba's deep sadness upon learning that his beloved wife, Ann, was unable to bear children—a revelation that had shaken him to his core.

In the solitude of his study, Zorba poured his heart onto the pages of his journal, his words a poignant reflection of his inner turmoil. He confessed his fears of loneliness and his desperate longing for a family of his own, a yearning that seemed destined to remain unfulfilled.

But amidst his despair, Zorba's mind turned to darker thoughts, thoughts of capturing and imprisoning souls within the confines of his mansion, a twisted attempt to fill the void left by his inability to have children. And so, one by one, he began to lure unsuspecting victims into his grasp, their spirits becoming ensnared within the walls of his macabre abode.

The first ghost he trapped was Emilio, the skilled chef whose culinary talents had once delighted guests at extravagant dinner parties. But beneath his jovial exterior lay a darkness—an abusive streak that had driven a wedge between him and his wife, condemning them both to an eternity of torment within the mansion's confines.

Next came the hanging lady, her spectral form suspended from the rafters of the mansion's grand hall. Once a servant girl in Zorba's employ, she had met a tragic end at the hands of her cruel master, her lifeless body left to swing in the breeze as a grim reminder of Zorba's brutality.

Shadrack the Headless Lion Tamer's Ghost was another unfortunate soul ensnared by Zorba's malevolent schemes. Once the star attraction of a traveling circus, Shadrack had met his untimely demise at the jaws of a ferocious beast, his decapitated head now forever lost to the void.

The wailing lady, clutching hands, and fiery skeleton each bore their own tragic tales of woe, their lives cut short by violence, betrayal, or despair. And the executioner, holding a severed head aloft, was a grim reminder of Zorba's insatiable thirst for power and control—a fate he had meted out to countless victims in his quest for dominance.

As Sullivan read through the journal, the stories of these lost souls unfolded before him, each one a testament to the depths of Zorba's depravity and the horrors that lay hidden within the mansion's shadowy corridors. And as the group listened in rapt silence, they couldn't help but feel a chill creeping into their bones—a foreboding sense of the darkness that awaited them in the haunted estate.

Silence hung heavy in the air, broken only by the soft rustle of pages as Sullivan delved deeper into Dr. Plato Zorba's journal. Each word seemed to cast a shadow over the room, the weight of Zorba's twisted thoughts and sinister deeds palpable in the dim light of the kitchen. The group sat in tense anticipation, their eyes fixed on Sullivan as he navigated the macabre labyrinth of Zorba's mind.

But as Sullivan reached the quarter mark of the journal, he suddenly stopped, his brow furrowing in deep concentration. His silence was deafening, a stark contrast to the eager anticipation that had filled the room only moments before. Concern etched itself into Nancy's features as she turned to Sullivan, her voice soft with worry.

"Are you okay, Professor?" she asked, her concern genuine as she reached out a comforting hand towards him. But Sullivan remained lost in thought, his gaze distant as he stared off into the distance, lost in the haunting words of Zorba's journal.

Finally, after what seemed like an eternity, Sullivan spoke, his voice low and somber as he broke the heavy silence that had settled over the group. "Dr. Plato Zorba was indeed a sick individual," he began, his words heavy with the weight of their implications. "As he aged, he found it more and more difficult to travel the world in search of ghosts to trap. Instead, he turned his attention to the unsuspecting victims right here in the surrounding area."

The revelation caused a creeping sense of dread of those gathered around the table, the realization sinking in like a lead weight in their stomachs. Zorba's twisted schemes had not been limited to the confines of his mansion—he had cast his net far and wide, ensnaring innocent souls in his quest for power and dominance.

As Sullivan continued to read from the journal, the group listened in stunned silence, their minds reeling from the horrors they were uncovering. The true extent of Zorba's depravity was slowly coming to light, each revelation more chilling than the last. And as they delved deeper into the darkness, they couldn't help but wonder what other horrors lay hidden within the pages of the journal—and what dangers awaited them in the haunted estate.

As Sullivan continued to leaf through the weathered pages of Dr. Plato Zorba's journal, a grim tableau of horror unfolded before his eyes. The entries chronicled Zorba's descent into madness, each word a chilling testament to the depths of his depravity and the atrocities he had committed in the name of power and control.

Among the most harrowing passages were those in which Zorba listed the names and ages of his victims—innocent souls whom he had lured into his clutches, their lives snuffed out in the blink of an eye. As Sullivan read aloud, the names echoed through the kitchen like a mournful dirge, each one a stark reminder of the lives lost to Zorba's insatiable hunger for dominance.

"Marie, aged 22... David, aged 16... Sarah, aged 30, Julie, aged 10..." Sullivan's voice faltered as he recited the names, each one etched into his memory like a scar upon his soul. The sheer number of victims was staggering, a testament to the depths of Zorba's depravity and the scale of his crimes.

But it was the ages of the victims that struck Sullivan the hardest—their youth and innocence robbed from them in the prime of their lives. As he read on, the weight of their lost potential hung heavy in the air, a haunting reminder of the lives cut short by Zorba's malevolent schemes.

As the group listened in stunned silence, the enormity of Zorba's crimes washed over them like a tidal wave of despair. Each name represented a tragedy, a life snuffed out before its time, and the weight of their collective loss bore down upon them like a crushing weight.

But amidst the darkness, a flicker of determination burned within Sullivan's heart. With each name he read, he vowed to honor the memory of Zorba's victims, to seek justice for their untimely deaths, and to ensure that their spirits found peace at last. And as he closed the journal, the resolve in his eyes was unmistakable—the battle against Zorba's darkness had only just begun.

CHAPTER TWENTY-THREE

As Sullivan closed the journal, the weight of its revelations casting a pall over the group gathered in the kitchen. But before anyone could speak, a sudden commotion erupted as Tiffany, overcome with emotion, began to tremble uncontrollably, her hands shaking as tears streamed down her cheeks.

The group watched in concern as Tiffany's distress escalated, her breaths coming in ragged gasps as she struggled to regain her composure. But before anyone could speak, a sudden commotion erupted as Tiffany, overcome with emotion, began to tremble uncontrollably, her hands shaking as tears streamed down her cheeks.

"Tiffany, what's wrong? Are you okay?"

But Tiffany could only shake her head, her words choked with emotion as she struggled to articulate the turmoil raging within her. Her mind raced with memories long buried, horrors she had spent a lifetime trying to forget. And as the weight of her past bore down upon her, she felt as though she were drowning in a sea of pain and despair.

Finally, as the storm within her began to subside, Tiffany found her voice, her words trembling with raw emotion as she addressed the group. "I-I need to tell you something," she began, her voice barely above a whisper. "Something I've never told anyone before."

With each word, Tiffany's story unfolded, a heartbreaking tale of abuse and neglect that had haunted her since childhood. She spoke of a father whose fists were as cruel as his words, of a mother who turned a blind eye to the horrors unfolding before her very eyes. She spoke of nights spent cowering in fear, of bruises hidden beneath long sleeves and forced smiles. Sexual abuse that she could not confide in anyone out of shame.

As she recounted her ordeal, the room fell silent, the weight of Tiffany's words hanging heavy in the air. The group listened in stunned silence, their hearts breaking with each new revelation. And as Tiffany's story drew to a close, the enormity of her pain washed over them like a tidal wave, leaving them reeling in its wake.

But amidst the darkness, a flicker of hope burned within Tiffany's eyes. For in sharing her story, she had reclaimed a piece of herself, a piece that had long been buried beneath the weight of her past. And as she looked around at the faces of her companions, she knew that she was not alone—that together, they would find the strength to face whatever horrors awaited them in the haunted estate.

Sullivan, his voice, calm and steady, cut through the tension that permeated the room, offering a glimmer of reassurance to his weary companions.

"While I had hoped that we would have found an exit from this place by now," Sullivan began, his gaze sweeping over the faces of his fellow survivors, "slowly but surely, I believe we are on the right track." His words carried a note of cautious optimism, a quiet determination to press on in the face of adversity.

Sullivan's suggestion of returning to their rooms and getting some much-needed rest was met with murmurs of agreement from the group. The trials of the day had taken their toll, both physically and mentally, and the prospect of a respite from the horrors of the haunted estate was a welcome one.

"Each of us should take this time to reflect on what we know and what we have experienced," Sullivan continued, his tone thoughtful as he addressed the group. "Perhaps with some brainstorming tomorrow, we will be able to devise a plan to escape this place once and for all."

The prospect of regrouping and strategizing filled the group with a renewed sense of purpose, a glimmer of hope amidst the encroaching darkness. As they made their way back to their rooms, the weight of the day's trials hung heavy on their shoulders, but beneath the weariness, there was a flicker of determination—a resolve to face whatever horrors awaited them with courage and conviction.

As Sullivan lay on his bed, his gaze fixed upon the ceiling, a swirl of thoughts and emotions churned within him like a tempestuous sea. Despite his years of experience in debunking charlatans and exposing the falsehoods of spiritualists and fortune tellers, nothing could have prepared him for the madness that now surrounded him and his group within the walls of the haunted estate.

The house, abandoned for over sixty years, had become a relic of the past—a forgotten monument to a bygone era. But beneath its crumbling facade lurked a darkness that defied rational explanation, a malevolent force that seemed to pulse with a life of its own.

As Sullivan pondered the events of the day, a nagging question gnawed at the corners of his mind: had their presence awakened the spirits that haunted the estate? It was a possibility, the implications too unsettling to contemplate.

According to some parapsychologists, the phenomenon of a "dead cell" occurred when a location remained dormant and devoid of paranormal activity for an extended period of time. But now, with their arrival, it seemed as though the slumbering spirits had been stirred from their centuries-old slumber, their restless souls awoken by the presence of the living.

The implications of this realization were staggering, the group now trapped within the confines of a house teeming with malevolent energy and vengeful spirits. With each passing moment, the darkness seemed to close in around them, suffocating their hopes of escape and leaving them at the mercy of forces beyond their comprehension.

But amidst the encroaching despair, a flicker of determination burned within Sullivan's heart. He refused to be cowed by the darkness that surrounded them, determined to uncover the truth behind the haunted estate and put an end to its reign of terror once and for all.

And as he closed his eyes and drifted into an uneasy sleep, the weight of their predicament weighed heavy on his mind, a constant reminder of the dangers that lurked within the shadows. For in the darkness of the night, the spirits of the estate whispered their secrets, their voices echoing through the halls with a chilling intensity that sent shivers down Sullivan's spine.

As Tiffany lay on her bed, her mind swirling with the echoes of her painful past, she tried to find solace in the darkness of her room. But sleep eluded her, her thoughts consumed by the specter of her own demons. Unaware of the danger that lurked in the shadows, she closed her eyes, hoping to find refuge in the embrace of sleep.

Suddenly, a chill swept through the room. If she had been awake, she would have noticed the telltale mist of her breath in the frigid air—a sign of the spectral presence that now hovered just beyond her field of vision.

Through the darkness, a figure materialized, its form twisted and contorted with malice. It was the ghost of Dr. Plato Zorba, his eyes burning with an otherworldly fire as he glided silently through the door, his intentions obscured by the veil of darkness that surrounded him.

Unaware of the danger that loomed above her, Tiffany remained lost in the depths of her troubled dreams, her slumber disturbed by the sinister presence that now hovered over her prone form. With a silent and deliberate movement, Zorba reached out, his ethereal fingers closing around a pillow at the foot of the bed.

In an instant, the air grew heavy with menace as Zorba's spectral form descended upon Tiffany, his intentions clear as he pressed the pillow down over her face, suffocating her in the darkness of the night. Terror gripped Tiffany's heart as she fought against the weight of the pillow, her screams muffled by the fabric that threatened to snuff out her very life.

But even as the darkness threatened to consume her, Tiffany found a strength she never knew she possessed—a defiance born of the horrors she had endured. With a surge of adrenaline, she tore the pillow away from her face, her eyes blazing with righteous anger as she confronted her attacker.

"I'm not afraid of you!" she screamed, her voice ringing out into the night with a ferocity that startled even herself. "You sick fuck!"

Zorba recoiled at her words, his spectral form writhing in agony as her gaze bore into him with an intensity that seemed to pierce the veil of his malevolent presence. With a final groan of defeat, he retreated, his form dissipating into the darkness as the rest of the group burst into the room, their faces pale with shock and concern.

As Tiffany gasped for breath, her heart racing with adrenaline, she knew that she had faced the darkness and emerged victorious. And as she looked around at the faces of her companions, she knew that she was not alone—that together, they would stand against the horrors that lurked within the haunted estate, united in their resolve to survive.

As Tiffany's heart raced and her breath came in ragged gasps, she clung to the edge of her bed, her hands trembling with adrenaline-fueled fear. But amidst the chaos of her terror, a spark of defiance ignited within her—a quiet resolve born of the horrors she had endured and the strength she had found within herself.

As she recounted her harrowing ordeal to the rest of the group, her voice trembled with raw emotion, but there was a newfound steel in her words—a determination to fight back against the darkness that threatened to consume her. "When I realized what Zorba was planning to do to me," she explained, her voice steady despite the tremors that still racked her body, "I found a calm presence within myself—a strength I didn't know I had."

With each word, Tiffany's resolve solidified, her mind racing with the beginnings of a plan to combat their spectral tormentor. She spoke of how, in the face of her attacker's malevolence, she had refused to be a victim—to cower in fear as she had in her youth. Instead, she had found the courage to stand up to Zorba, to confront him with the defiant proclamation that she was not afraid.

And as she recounted the moment when Zorba's spectral form had faltered, stunned by her words, she knew that she had struck a chord—a weakness in her assailant's armor that they could exploit. "When I told him I wasn't afraid," she continued, her voice tinged with a newfound sense of determination, "it seemed to stun him. And that's when he disappeared."

The rest of the group listened in stunned silence, their eyes wide with realization as Tiffany's words sank in. If they could exploit Zorba's fear of the strong and defiant, they might stand a chance of turning the tables on their spectral adversary. With each passing moment, their resolve solidified, their determination to survive growing stronger with every beat of their hearts.

And as they huddled together in the darkness of Tiffany's room, a plan began to take shape—a plan to confront the darkness head-on, armed with nothing but their courage and their unwavering determination to survive. For in the face of the horrors that lurked within the haunted estate, they knew that their only hope lay in standing together, united in their defiance against the forces of darkness that sought to destroy them.

CHAPTER TWENTY-FOUR

As THE GROUP gathered in the kitchen, each member was grappling with the danger of their situation. Sullivan, ever the voice of reason and skepticism, hesitated before speaking, his mind racing with conflicting thoughts and emotions.

"I know this may sound... unorthodox," Sullivan began, his voice measured as he addressed the group, "but considering the circumstances, I believe it may be worth exploring avenues that I once dismissed as mere superstition."

His words were met with a mixture of surprise and uncertainty from the rest of the group, their eyes fixed on him with a mixture of curiosity and apprehension. For years, Sullivan had been a staunch skeptic, his work focused on exposing the fraudulent practices of those who claimed to possess supernatural abilities.

"But," Sullivan continued, his gaze shifting to Tiffany, "given what we've experienced and what Tiffany has revealed to us, I can't help but feel that there may be more to the occult than I previously thought. Perhaps... there is a method to the madness, a way to harness the energies of this place for our own purposes."

"What do you mean, Professor?" asked Stu as the others looked on.

"I'm suggesting that we hold a séance," he replied.

The suggestion of holding a seance and its implications both tantalized and terrified the group. For Sullivan, it was a departure from everything he thought he knew about the occult—a realm he had long regarded with skepticism and disdain. But now, faced with the reality of the haunted estate and the malevolent forces that lurked within, he couldn't help but entertain the possibility that there might be more to it than meets the eye.

"And if there's even a chance," Sullivan continued, his voice tinged with a hint of uncertainty, "that we can communicate with the spirits trapped within this place, perhaps we can find a way to help them—and ourselves—in the process."

With that, the group fell into a thoughtful silence, the weight of Sullivan's words hanging heavy in the air. It was a risky proposition, fraught with uncertainty and danger, but it was also their best chance at unraveling the mysteries of the haunted estate and putting an end to the darkness that threatened to consume them all.

"Tiffany," Sullivan's voice cut through the tense silence like a knife, his words laden with a sense of urgency that sent a shiver down the group's collective spine. "The more I process the events we have all experienced, the more I feel you are the possible conduit to the spirits who reside in this estate."

His eyes bore into Tiffany's, their intensity reflecting the gravity of the situation they found themselves in. The weight of his words hung heavy in the air, each syllable pregnant with the weight of the unknown.

"Of all of us here, you appear to be the most qualified to establish a connection with the spirits trapped in the house with us," Sullivan continued, his voice low and urgent. "But, I must caution you and everyone. So far, the only life-threatening spirit is that of Dr. Plato Zorba."

A chill settled over the group as Sullivan's words sank in, the reality of their predicament casting a pall over their hopes of finding a solution. The specter of Zorba loomed large in their minds, his malevolent presence a constant reminder of the dangers that lurked within the haunted estate.

"But once we reach out to the spirits contained here," Sullivan's voice dropped to a whisper, his gaze sweeping over the group with a mixture of apprehension and determination, "we do not know if other dangerous apparitions might appear, putting Tiffany's life in danger."

The gravity of Sullivan's warning hung in the air like a dark cloud, each member of the group acutely aware of the risks they faced in their pursuit of answers. But amidst the uncertainty and fear, there was a glimmer of hope—a determination to confront the darkness head-on and emerge victorious against the malevolent forces that sought to destroy them.

As Sullivan's cautionary words reverberated through the room, Tiffany felt a surge of apprehension coursing through her veins, her heart pounding in her chest as she grappled with the gravity of the situation. The weight of Sullivan's warning hung heavy in the air, casting a shadow over her hopes of finding a solution to their plight.

For a moment, Tiffany hesitated, her mind racing with a thousand thoughts and fears. The specter of Dr. Plato Zorba loomed large in her mind, his malevolent presence a constant reminder of the dangers that lurked within the haunted estate. The idea of reaching out to the spirits trapped within the house filled her with a sense of unease, a nagging voice of doubt whispering in the back of her mind.

But as she looked around at the faces of her companions, their eyes filled with a mixture of uncertainty and determination, Tiffany felt a flicker of resolve stirring within her. Despite the risks, despite the unknown dangers that awaited them, she knew that they had to try. They couldn't let fear dictate their actions—not when the lives of so many innocent souls hung in the balance.

With a deep breath, Tiffany squared her shoulders, her gaze meeting Sullivan's with a steely determination. "I understand the risks," she said, her voice steady despite the tremors that still lingered beneath the surface. "But if there's even a chance that we can help those trapped spirits—and put an end to Zorba's reign of terror—then I'm willing to try."

Her words hung in the air, a silent vow of defiance against the darkness that threatened to consume them all. And as she prepared herself for the seance that lay ahead, Tiffany knew that she was ready to face whatever dangers awaited them, armed with nothing but her courage and her unwavering determination to see their mission through to the end.

"Where do you want to hold it, Professor?" Nancy asked.

Nancy's question lingered, drawing the group's attention to Sullivan, who paused thoughtfully before responding.

"I believe we should hold the seance in Ann Zorba's room," he said, his tone serious. "The strained relationship between Ann and Plato Zorba before her tragic end suggests it's an area of the house he avoids."

Sullivan's suggestion cast a solemn shadow over their discussion, emphasizing the gravity of their task. Ann Zorba's room, steeped in the echoes of past anguish, held the potential to unveil secrets long hidden within the estate's walls.

With Sullivan's proposal, the group faced a pivotal decision, one that could lead them closer to understanding the estate's dark history—or plunge them deeper into its sinister depths. As they prepared to navigate the treacherous terrain of the unknown, they braced themselves for the challenges that lay ahead, united in their resolve to confront the darkness and emerge victorious.

Sullivan's gaze swept across the group, his expression expectant as he awaited their response. "Is everyone in agreement?" he inquired, his voice steady despite the undercurrent of tension that permeated the room.

Thomas was the first to speak up, his voice resolute as he addressed the group. "I think it is up to Tiffany," he stated firmly, his words echoed by nods of agreement from the others.

Tiffany, sensing the weight of the decision resting on her shoulders, met their gazes with a steely determination. "I'm up for it," she affirmed, her voice steady despite the nervous fluttering in her chest. "Especially if it leads to us getting out of this house."

Sullivan nodded in approval, his gaze lingering on each member of the group in turn. "Very well," he said, his tone decisive. "Nancy, Stu, you two have more experience with seances than any of us. We'll need a round table to start with. Once we find one, gather some candles."

Turning to the others, Sullivan continued, his instructions clear and concise. "Stu, Thomas, Jeff—gather up some equipment and bring it to the room. If possible, I'd like to record all the activity that takes place during the seance."

With their roles assigned and their preparations underway, the group set about their task with a sense of purpose and determination. As they worked together to assemble the necessary supplies and make the final preparations, a palpable sense of anticipation hung in the air, each member of the group steeling themselves for the challenges that lay ahead.

CHAPTER TWENTY-FIVE

STU AND NANCY surveyed Ann's room with a critical eye, ensuring that every detail was in place for the upcoming seance. "I think we've set up the room similarly to the ones Nancy and I have attended," Stu remarked, his voice filled with confidence. "Minus the crystal ball, and we're all set," he added, a hint of satisfaction coloring his words.

Tiffany, feeling a mixture of excitement and nervousness, turned to the group for guidance. "What do I say or do?" she asked, her voice tinged with uncertainty.

Sullivan considered her question for a moment before responding. "Nancy, why don't you explain to Tiffany how those fake spiritualists summon the dead," he suggested, his gaze shifting between the two women. "I don't think there's a prescribed script for this," he added, emphasizing the need for authenticity and spontaneity in their approach.

Nancy nodded in agreement, her expression serious as she turned to Tiffany. "It's all about creating a connection with the spirits," she explained, her voice gentle yet firm. "You'll want to speak from the heart, using whatever words feel right in the moment. Trust your instincts, and remember that we're all here to support you."

Tiffany absorbed Nancy's words, a sense of determination settling over her as she prepared herself for the task ahead. With the guidance of her companions and the strength of their collective resolve behind her, she felt ready to face whatever challenges the seance might bring.

"Stu, Nancy, shall we take our seats?" Sullivan's voice echoed through the dimly lit room, the anticipation thick in the air like a tangible presence.

"Yes, and when you are seated, I will light a candle and place it in the center of the table," Nancy's instructions rang out, her voice steady despite the underlying tension. Each word seemed to hang in the air, weighted with the gravity of the task ahead. "Everyone should place their hands on the table and touch a finger to the one next to you, forming a circle," she continued, her movements deliberate as she demonstrated, touching Stu's baby finger on one side and Tiffany's on the other. "Whatever happens, do not break the circle," she added, her tone firm, a warning underscored by the seriousness of their situation.

As the group settled into their seats, a hush fell over the room, broken only by the soft flicker of candlelight casting eerie shadows on the walls. With each passing moment, the tension grew, the weight of their collective expectations bearing down on them like a heavy blanket.

Sullivan exchanged a meaningful glance with Nancy and Stu, his expression a mixture of determination and apprehension. They were about to embark on a journey into the unknown, where the boundaries between the living and the dead blurred and reality itself seemed to shift and warp.

With a steadying breath, Sullivan took his place at the table, his heart pounding in his chest as he braced himself for whatever lay ahead. Around him, the others followed suit, their hands trembling slightly as they formed the circle, their fingers touching in a silent vow of solidarity.

And as Nancy lit the candle, its flame casting dancing shadows across their faces, the group braced themselves for the unknown, ready to confront the darkness that lurked within the haunted estate and emerge victorious against the malevolent forces that sought to destroy them.

As the group settled into their seats, a heavy silence descended upon the room, punctuated only by the soft flicker of candlelight casting eerie shadows on the walls. Minutes passed, each one stretching into an eternity as they waited with bated breath for something—anything—to happen.

Tiffany, her eyes half-closed in concentration, seemed to drift into a trance-like state, her breathing slow and steady as if she were on the cusp of some profound revelation. The others watched in tense anticipation, their hearts pounding in their chests as they waited for the moment when the veil between the living and the dead would be pierced.

Suddenly, without warning, the candle in the center of the table sputtered and went out, plunging the room into darkness. A collective gasp escaped the group as they stared into the blackness, their senses heightened in the absence of light.

And then, as if summoned by some unseen force, a faint glow began to emanate from the center of the table. At first, it was barely discernible—a soft, ethereal light that seemed to shimmer and dance in the darkness.

As the glow intensified, a figure began to materialize—a spectral form rising slowly from the center of the table, its features obscured by a halo of light. It was the ghost of Ann Zorba, her form translucent and otherworldly as she hovered in the air, her gaze fixed on the group with an intensity that sent shivers down their spines.

But she was not alone.

As Ann Zorba began to rise towards the ceiling, she was joined by numerous other entities—ghostly apparitions, their forms twisted and grotesque from years of torture at the hands of Plato Zorba. Their faces contorted in agony, their eyes hollow and vacant as they drifted upwards, drawn towards the ceiling like moths to a flame.

The room filled with an eerie chorus of moans and wails, the sound of tortured souls crying out in anguish as they ascended towards the heavens. And as the last of the apparitions disappeared into the darkness above, the group was left staring into the void, their minds reeling with the enormity of what they had just witnessed.

As the young ghosts circled around Tiffany, their spectral forms shimmering in the dim light, a sense of urgency filled the air. Their voices, faint and ethereal, echoed in her mind, pleading for help, their words a haunting refrain that sent shivers down her spine.

"We're trapped," one of the ghosts murmured, its voice tinged with desperation. "Please, you have to help us. We can't escape this house on our own."

Tiffany felt a surge of compassion welling up inside her, her heart aching at the sight of these tortured souls condemned to wander the halls of the mansion for all eternity. She reached out a trembling hand, her fingers brushing against the cool, insubstantial form of the nearest ghost.

"I'll do everything I can to help you," she whispered, her voice filled with determination. "We'll find a way to break free from this place together."

The ghosts hovered around her, their presence a tangible reminder of the darkness that lurked within the haunted estate. But despite the fear that gripped her heart, Tiffany refused to back down. With the support of her companions and the strength of her own resolve, she would do whatever it took to bring an end to the suffering of these lost souls and find a way to escape the house once and for all.

As the young ghosts circled around Tiffany, their voices pleading for help, a sudden tremor shook the room, sending a wave of panic through the group. The floor beneath them rumbled and quaked, the walls groaning in protest as pictures fell from their hooks and Ann's mirror on her dresser cracked with a resounding shatter.

"Stay in the circle!" Nancy shouted, her voice barely audible over the din of the room. "Don't break the circle!"

Tiffany clung to the hands of her companions, her heart pounding in her chest as the room continued to shake violently around them. The ghosts cried out in alarm, their voices mingling with the chaos as they warned of his impending arrival—the ghost of Zorba, their tormentor.

"He's coming!" they cried, their words a chilling refrain that sent a shiver down Tiffany's spine. And then, as suddenly as they had appeared, the ghosts vanished, leaving behind an eerie silence that hung heavy in the air.

With quick reflexes, Sullivan broke the circle and lit the candle once more, the flickering flame casting a soft glow that illuminated the room. Nancy rushed to Tiffany's side, her hands gentle as she brought her out of her trance, the shaking in the room gradually coming to a stop.

As the group caught their breath and took stock of their surroundings, a sense of unease lingered in the air. They had narrowly escaped the clutches of Zorba's ghost, but they knew that their ordeal was far from over. With determination in their hearts and unity in their ranks, they braced themselves for the challenges that lay ahead, ready to confront the darkness and emerge victorious against the malevolent forces that sought to destroy them.

CHAPTER TWENTY-SIX

THE GROUP HURRIED back to the kitchen, their hearts pounding with adrenaline-fueled urgency. Stu and Jeff wasted no time in reviewing the recordings they had painstakingly captured. As anticipated, Ann's spectral presence manifested, sending a chill through the room that seemed to seep into their bones, lingering until the last of the apparitions dissipated. However, to their disappointment, the footage only revealed blurry, indistinct specters, frustratingly elusive in their clarity.

Tiffany, feeling parched from the tension of the encounter, requested water and nearly drained an entire bottle in one gulp. "What are your thoughts, Professor?" Nancy inquired, concern etched into her voice as she approached Sullivan.

Sullivan's expression betrayed his inner turmoil. "I must admit, I am somewhat disappointed," he confessed, his voice heavy with regret. "I inadvertently placed Tiffany's life in jeopardy, yet what have we truly gleaned from this séance?" Overhearing the conversation, Tiffany joined them, her demeanor surprisingly composed.

"Actually, I believe I've gained valuable insights," she interjected, her tone earnest. "During my trance, I experienced a profound sense of panic, but it abated when the spirits of the young victims communicated with me."

Sullivan's skepticism wavered slightly as Tiffany's words sank in, mingling with a burgeoning sense of curiosity. "It's intriguing," he mused, his brow furrowing deeper as he pondered her revelation. "So, you felt a connection to them? A shared understanding of past traumas?"

Tiffany nodded earnestly, her eyes reflecting the weight of her experience. "Yes, exactly," she affirmed, her voice tinged with a mixture of awe and apprehension. "It was as though they sensed the pain I carried from my own childhood, the echoes of abuse lingering in the shadows of my memory. And they... they wanted me to help them find peace, to release them from the shackles of this accursed house."

A shiver ran down Nancy's spine as she absorbed Tiffany's words, the gravity of their situation sinking in with chilling clarity. "So, what now?" she asked, her voice trembling slightly with uncertainty. The house seemed to creak and groan, its very walls pulsating with an undercurrent of anger, as if Zorba himself resented their intrusion into his domain.

"The ghosts," Tiffany began, her voice trembling slightly, "they told me that in the back of Zorba's journal we found, there lies a chant. A chant he utilized to ensnare ghosts before bringing them to this accursed place." Her words were met with a collective intake of breath, the group's eyes widening in realization of the implications.

"He used that same chant," Tiffany continued, her tone heavy with solemnity, "to bind these restless souls to the confines of this house, even after their passing. It's how he maintains his twisted dominion over them." The revelation hung in the air like a dark cloud, casting a shadow over their hopes of escape.

"But," she interjected, her voice gaining strength with newfound determination, "if we can locate that chant, perhaps we can turn it against him. Break the chains that bind these spirits and put an end to Zorba's reign of terror once and for all."

A sense of resolve settled over the group as they exchanged determined glances, united in their newfound purpose. Yet, as they braced themselves for the trials that lay ahead, the house seemed to echo with the furious protests of Zorba himself, his anger palpable in every groan and creak that reverberated through its ancient halls. They knew that their path would not be easy, but they were determined to confront the darkness head-on and reclaim their freedom from the clutches of this malevolent entity.

Sullivan's hands moved with urgency as he snatched the journal, flipping through its pages in a desperate search for the elusive chant. His disappointment was obvious as he reached the end, finding nothing but empty pages staring back at him. "There is nothing here," he muttered, his voice heavy with frustration. "I wonder if they are referring to the other journals Francis Zorba gave to me."

"May I take a look, Professor?" Nancy's voice cut through the air, her curiosity piqued by the possibility of uncovering hidden secrets. Sullivan handed the journal to her without hesitation, his eyes alight with a glimmer of hope.

Nancy examined the journal with meticulous care, scrutinizing every detail in search of any hidden clues. Her fingers traced the edges of the front cover, then trailed along the spine to the back, her brows furrowing in concentration. Just as she was about to concede defeat, her gaze landed on a seemingly innocuous detail.

"Wait a minute," she exclaimed, a spark of excitement igniting in her eyes. "Look here." She pointed to the small left-hand corner of the journal, where a subtle irregularity caught her attention. It appeared as though someone had carefully peeled back a portion of the page, only to conceal it with a thin layer of wax, seamlessly blending it into the surrounding paper.

The discovery sent a ripple of anticipation through the group as they gathered around, eager to uncover the secrets hidden beneath the surface. With trembling fingers, Nancy carefully peeled away the layer of wax, revealing a hidden compartment nestled within the journal's pages. Within it lay a piece of parchment, its surface adorned with intricate symbols and ancient runes, faintly illuminated by the flickering candlelight.

As they gazed upon the mysterious inscription, a sense of determination filled the room. They knew that this was their key to unlocking the mysteries of Zorba's dark magic, and with it, they would finally have the means to confront the malevolent forces that held them captive within the haunted mansion.

"It looks like Latin," Sullivan observed, squinting as he attempted to decipher the intricate symbols adorning the parchment. "We'll need better lighting to read this properly. Let's head back to the entrance hall; the illumination there should serve us well," he suggested, his voice firm with resolve.

The group nodded in agreement, their anticipation mounting as they prepared to unravel the secrets concealed within the ancient text. With cautious steps, they retraced their path through the dimly lit corridors of the mansion, the oppressive atmosphere seemingly growing heavier with each passing moment.

As they reached the entrance hall, a wave of relief washed over them at the sight of the grand chandeliers suspended from the ceiling, casting a warm, golden glow across the room. Sullivan positioned himself beneath the nearest fixture, the light bathing the parchment in a soft, ambient glow.

With renewed determination, he began to pore over the inscription, his brow furrowing in concentration as he translated the cryptic words into comprehensible language. Each syllable carried the weight of centuries-old knowledge, hinting at the dark magic that had been wielded within these walls.

As the translation unfolded, a sense of unease settled over the group, the gravity of their discovery weighing heavily upon them. Yet, they knew that they were on the brink of uncovering the key to unlocking Zorba's sinister machinations, and with it, the possibility of freeing themselves from his malevolent grasp.

With bated breath, they awaited Sullivan's revelation, knowing that their journey was far from over and that the true test of their courage and resilience lay ahead.

"There are actually two chants here," Sullivan said as he attempted to translate them. One he used have used to trap the ghosts here. The other one is how to free them."

"Can you read them, Professor?" Tiffany asked. Sullivan nodded and the group gathered around.

"Chant to Retain a Ghost:

In noctem tenebris, umbrae silentes,
Invoco te, spiritus errantes.
Vinculum aeternum, nex arcanae,
Adhaeret aeternum, mors oblitae.
Mortem non excita, corpus retine,
Spiritus vinculis, terram cohibe.
In manibus tenebris, custodire,
In umbrae silentis, manere.

"That's great. What the hell does that mean?" Thomas asked

"It means, Thomas:

In the night of darkness, silent shadows,
I invoke thee, wandering spirits.
Eternal bond, arcane ties,
Bound forever, death forgotten.
Awaken not death, retain the body,
Bind the spirit, confine to earth.
In the hands of darkness, guard,
In the silent shadows, abide.

"Well, the heck with that one. We need to free the other spirits and get out of here," Nancy said excitedly.

"Yes. Okay. The second reads,

Chant to Free a Ghost:

Ex tenebris, liberatio,
Spiritus liberi, liberare.
Vincula rupta, nex solutus,
Ad astra redeunt, libertate fruere.
Mors excita, animam revocare,
Spiritus solutus, in aeternum vagare.
In lucem aeternam, liberatio,
In libertate aeterna, redire.

"This means:

From darkness, liberation,
Free the spirit, to be freed.
Bonds broken, ties undone,
Return to the stars, enjoy freedom.
Awaken death, call back the soul,
Spirit released, wander forever.
Into eternal light, liberation,
In eternal freedom, return.

CHAPTER TWENTY-SEVEN

As Sullivan completed the translation of the ancient chant, a sudden sense of foreboding descended upon the group, as if they had unwittingly unleashed a dormant force lurking within the very fabric of the house. Before they could react, all hell broke loose.

With a deafening roar, the walls of the mansion began to crack and splinter, as if unable to contain the fury that raged within. Lights flickered and danced erratically, illuminating corridors that had long been shrouded in darkness. Objects trembled and crashed to the ground, their descent accompanied by the cacophony of screams echoing through the haunted halls.

In the blink of an eye, mold began to creep and crawl across the walls, spreading like a malignant plague devouring everything in its path. The air grew thick with a sickening stench, a putrid odor that invaded their senses and churned their stomachs with its malevolence.

It was unmistakable—the spirit of Dr. Plato Zorba was enraged, his wrath manifesting in the chaotic upheaval that consumed the house. With every tremor and every scream, they felt his presence looming over them like a specter of doom, a reminder of the darkness that lurked within the mansion's walls.

Terrified yet resolute, the group braced themselves against the onslaught, knowing that they had unleashed forces beyond their control. As the chaos raged around them, they steeled their resolve, determined to confront Zorba's wrath head-on and put an end to the horrors that haunted them once and for all.

The urgency in Sullivan's voice cut through the chaos like a beacon of clarity, rallying the group amidst the turmoil that engulfed them. "Quick, we must retreat to the lower floor and commence the chant," he urged, his words laced with a sense of impending doom. "Tiffany, you must recite the chant. The rest of us will surround you, shielding you from Zorba's grasp. Let us waste no time."

With hearts pounding and adrenaline coursing through their veins, the group hastily descended the creaking staircase, their footsteps echoing in sync with the thunderous tremors that reverberated through the house. Each step felt like a battle against the suffocating grip of fear, their senses heightened to the point of hypersensitivity as they braced themselves for the confrontation that awaited them below.

Reaching the lower floor, they formed a protective circle around Tiffany, their eyes darting nervously to every shadow that danced in the beams of their flashlights. The air crackled with tension as they prepared to begin the incantation, their voices trembling with a mixture of apprehension and determination.

As Tiffany took a steadying breath and began to recite the ancient chant while Nancy held her flashlight over the words. The words carried with them the weight of centuries-old magic and the hope of salvation. The group held their breath, their gazes locked in unwavering focus as they awaited the outcome of their desperate gambit.

Outside, the storm raged on, its fury matched only by the turmoil that writhed within the haunted mansion. But within the protective circle they had formed, a flicker of defiance burned bright, a beacon of resistance against the encroaching darkness that threatened to consume them all. With each verse of the chant, they felt the oppressive grip of Zorba's wrath begin to loosen, his power waning in the face of their unity and resolve.

The door leading to the lower level swung open with a resounding creak, only to be violently slammed shut by an unseen force. Zorba's spectral form manifested, his anguished curses and unearthly screams echoing through the chamber with chilling intensity. Undeterred by the cacophony of chaos, Tiffany pressed on, her voice steady as she continued to recite the ancient chant, each word a beacon of defiance against the encroaching darkness.

As the tension in the room reached its zenith, the temperature plummeted, causing everyone to shiver. Amidst the eerie symphony of ghostly sounds, the storm outside intensified, its thunderous roars and jagged bolts of lightning serving as a chilling backdrop to the unfolding confrontation.

Suddenly, as if guided by some malevolent force, the beams of everyone's flashlights flickered and died, plunging the dungeon into suffocating darkness. Nancy's terrified scream pierced the silence, but Tiffany, her resolve unshaken, continued to recite the chant by heart, her words a beacon of hope amidst the encroaching gloom.

In the darkness, a massive hand, the hand of Zorba himself, emerged from the wall, followed by the grotesque form of the enraged spirit. With a primal roar, he lashed out at the protective barrier surrounding Tiffany, his fury palpable in every movement. Yet still, she persisted, her voice unwavering as she continued to recite the chant with unwavering determination.

The air crackled with raw energy as the confrontation reached its climax, the forces of light and darkness locked in a desperate struggle for supremacy. But in the face of Zorba's wrath, Tiffany stood resolute, her unwavering faith in the power of the chant serving as a beacon of hope amidst the encroaching darkness. And as she continued to recite the ancient words, a flicker of light pierced the darkness, illuminating the chamber with a radiant glow of hope.

As the confrontation reached its climax, a remarkable transformation began to unfold within the chamber. The combined efforts of Zorba's wife, Ann, and the other young spirits gathered momentum, their collective strength slowly chipping away at the malevolent entity that was Zorba.

A radiant light began to emanate from an unseen source, its brilliance growing with each passing moment. Even Zorba, in all his fury, was compelled to turn away from Tiffany and the group, his gaze drawn inexorably towards the burgeoning glow.

The first apparition to emerge from the stone floor was that of Ann Zorba, her spectral form ethereal yet resolute. Behind her, a multitude of young children and adult spirits materialized, their presence a testament to the unity and determination of the oppressed souls bound by Zorba's tyranny.

In a final act of desperation, Zorba lashed out over the heads of the group, trying to strike Tiffany with a brutal force, which she avoids. "We are not afraid of you anymore. We are not afraid of you anymore," she added with the chant. In response, the ghostly apparitions unleashed a torrent of rage upon Zorba, their collective fury overwhelming even the most potent of defenses.

Though Zorba attempted to ward off their onslaught, his efforts were in vain against the relentless assault of the vengeful spirits. As they darted in and out of his spectral form, tearing away at his essence with relentless determination, parts of his apparition began to break away, replaced by the brilliant glow of pure light.

In a stunning display of triumph over darkness, the combined efforts of Ann and the other spirits proved victorious, their unwavering resolve breaking Zorba apart piece by piece until all that remained was the radiant glow of liberation, casting out the shadows that had long plagued the haunted mansion.

The group's focus shifts to Tiffany, sprawled on the floor. Sullivan checks for a pulse. "She's not breathing," he announces, his voice tense. "Give me some space." He begins CPR, but it proves futile. Tiffany is gone. As Sullivan rises to offer condolences to the group, their astonishment mounts as a warm glow emanates from Tiffany's body. Her mortal form becomes increasingly transparent until it vanishes, morphing into a spectral presence that hovers above her lifeless shell.

"Do not be saddened," Tiffany's voice, now ghostly and ethereal, reverberates through the chamber. "I am finally at peace. Our actions have liberated the spirits. Dr. Plato Zorba is vanquished."

Nancy's sobs echoed through the chamber. Stu, Jeff, and Thomas stood frozen in shock, the swirling apparitions of the spirits rendering them awestruck and uncertain of what to do next.

"Thank you, Tiffany. Thank you," the voices of the spirits murmured, a chorus of gratitude swirling around the room .

As Tiffany ascended into the air, surrounded by the liberated spirits who danced with joy at their newfound freedom, a section of the stone wall crumbled, revealing a cache of hidden wealth. Stu's eyes widened in disbelief as he beheld the treasure trove before them. "It's the rest of Dr. Zorba's money he hid," he exclaimed, his voice tinged with awe. "There must be over a million dollars here."

But for Sullivan and Nancy, the riches held no allure. Their focus remained fixed on Tiffany's transcendent departure, a beacon of light amidst the darkness that had plagued them for so long.

"It is time for us to leave," Tiffany's spirit declared, as a luminous opening appeared in the ceiling, bathing the chamber in radiant light. One by one, the spirits departed, their joyous exodus a testament to the victory they had achieved together.

The group quietly climbs the stairs back to the grand entrance, one person less. Thomas again, is the last person on the ladder. With tears streaming down his cheeks, Thomas turns his gaze on the torture chamber one last time. "Rest in hell, Dr. Plato Zorba," he whispered, his voice trembling with a mixture of grief and triumph.

CHAPTER TWENTY-EIGHT

IN THE SOMBER aftermath of Tiffany's passing, a heavy silence enveloped the group. Each member grappling with their own emotions, their thoughts consumed by the gravity of the moment.

Meanwhile, Jeff, seeking a sense of normalcy amidst the chaos, made his way to where the equipment was stored, his footsteps echoing softly in the cavernous space. With practiced efficiency, he checked the readings, his brow furrowing in concentration as he studied the monitors.

Sensing that the moment was ripe for revelation, Jeff caught Sullivan's attention, gesturing towards the readouts with a solemn expression. "Professor," he said softly, his voice barely rising above a whisper. "There is no longer any activity being recorded in the house."

His words hung in the air, a stark contrast to the tumultuous events that had transpired mere moments ago. In the absence of the supernatural disturbances that had plagued them, a sense of eerie calm settled over the mansion, its once-haunted halls now eerily still.

With an eerie creak, the imposing double entry doors swung open, as if propelled by an otherworldly force. In their wake, the remaining windows, still adorned with tattered drapes, were torn from their moorings, crashing to the ground with a resounding thud. Sunlight flooded into the once-shadowed foyer, banishing the lingering gloom that had shrouded the mansion and dispelling the remnants of the storm that had raged outside.

Despite the newfound brightness and the beckoning call of freedom beyond the threshold, none among the group made a move to leave. The significance of the moment hung heavy in the air, a silent acknowledgment of the bond they shared and the sacrifice Tiffany had made. And so, they stood together in silent vigil, unwilling to depart from the house they had all previously yearned to escape.

ONE WEEK LATER:

As the group dressed in black gathers outside the estate, near the foot of the stairs leading into the house, a black Mercedes Benz pulls up, and Francis Zorba steps out. She recognizes the somber atmosphere and realizes the group is there to share a final moment with the spirit of Tiffany, so she waits respectfully for them to finish.

Nancy steps forward and places a white rose on the step, a silent tribute to their departed friend. After a few moments of silence, the group turns to leave, and Sullivan approaches Zorba.

"Professor Sullivan," Zorba begins, her voice carrying a solemn tone, "I want to express my deepest condolences for your loss. I understand Tiffany was a remarkable young woman, and her bravery will not be forgotten."

Sullivan nods, his expression reflecting gratitude for the sentiment. "Thank you, Ms. Zorba. Tiffany's spirit will always hold a special place in all our heart."

Sullivan then addresses the matter of the estate, his voice carrying a weight of revelation, "We discovered a considerable amount of money within the house. Apparently what Benjamin Rush found sixty years ago was only part of the fortune your great uncle concealed in the house."

Zorba nods in understanding. "Yes, I suspected there might be more. I've decided to donate it to the university's psychology department who will set up a scholarship fund for future students. I've decided to call it the Tiffany Fund, in honor of her memory. I hope that is alright with you?"

Sullivan's expression is touched by the gesture. "That's more than alright, Ms. Zorba. It's a beautiful tribute." Curiosity flickers in his eyes. "And what of the house? What do you plan to do with it?"

Zorba's gaze turns to the imposing structure behind them, her expression contemplative. "A demolition crew will arrive this week to tear it down. In its place, condominiums will be built, and also a new school bringing new life to this land."

Sullivan absorbs this information with a mixture of relief and acceptance. "It's for the best," he murmurs, a sense of closure settling over him.

"I believe these belong to you," he said as he handed Zorba the pair of special glasses. After looking at them, she violently threw them to the ground, breaking them into numerous pieces, her action reflecting a final release from the haunted past.

With a final nod of acknowledgment, Zorba and the group bid farewell to the haunted estate and the memories it holds, ready to embrace the future with renewed hope and resolve, their hearts lighter as they step away from the shadows of the past into the brightness of a new beginning.

As the group bids their final farewells to the haunted estate, a sense of closure settles over them like a comforting shroud. Each step away from the mansion feels like a release from the grip of the past, a step towards the promise of a brighter future. Yet, as they turn to leave, a subtle shift in the atmosphere draws their attention upward.

High above, on the highest part of the mansion's structure, a figure emerges from the shadows. It's Tiffany's spirit, ethereal and luminous, looking down upon them with a gentle gaze. Her presence radiates a sense of peace and reassurance, a silent reminder that she will always be with them, even as they move forward into the unknown.

The group pauses, captivated by the sight of their departed friend, bathed in the soft glow of twilight. It's as if time stands still in that moment, suspended between the realms of the living and the dead. Memories of their time together flood their minds, mingling with the bittersweet realization that Tiffany's spirit will forever linger in the halls of the mansion.

Nancy's eyes brim with tears, a mixture of sorrow and gratitude as she gazes up at Tiffany. Stu and Thomas exchange solemn nods, silently acknowledging the profound impact Tiffany had on their lives. Jeff's expression softens with a sense of closure, knowing that Tiffany's spirit will always watch over them even after the house is demolished.

Sullivan, too, is moved by the sight of Tiffany's spirit, his heart heavy with both loss and reverence. He raises a hand in a silent farewell, his lips forming a whispered thank you to the heavens above. For a moment, it feels as though Tiffany is reaching out to them, bridging the gap between the living and the dead with her boundless love and unwavering presence.

With a final, lingering glance at Tiffany's spectral form, the group continues on their journey, hearts lighter and spirits lifted by the knowledge that they carry a piece of Tiffany's spirit with them wherever they go. And as they fade into the distance, Tiffany's luminous figure remains, a beacon of light amidst the darkness, a symbol of hope and resilience in the face of adversity.

EPILOGUE

Francis Zorba remained true to her word. The funds discovered within the mansion were allocated to demolish the estate, paving the way for the creation of a stunning condominium community. Adjacent to this development, the community now boasts both an elementary and middle school, enriching the area's educational opportunities. An expansive park, named Tiffany Park, graces the landscape, complete with a serene pond, enhancing the area's natural beauty.

Furthermore, the establishment of the Tiffany Scholarship Fund provided a lifeline for students who had overcome adversity. This initiative empowered countless at-risk individuals to turn their lives around. Remarkably, every recipient of the scholarship has gone on to successfully graduate from their chosen colleges or trade schools, embodying the transformative power of opportunity.

Jeff pursued his passion for technology, culminating in the attainment of his Ph.D. He currently resides in Santa Clara, California, where he contributes his expertise to a prominent high-tech firm in Silicon Valley. Alongside his professional achievements, Jeff found love with a high school teacher, and together they are raising two wonderful children, enriching their lives with love and laughter.

Thomas encountered a life-altering event when he was involved in a harrowing traffic accident, resulting in a debilitating back injury that dashed his dreams of NFL stardom. Undeterred by adversity, he redirected his focus towards coaching and now serves as a defensive coach at a prestigious university on the east coast. With unwavering determination, Thomas harbors aspirations of coaching at the professional level, fueled by his passion for the game and his resilient spirit.

Nancy's academic journey led her to graduate with honors and earn a Master's degree in Children Family Counseling. She dedicated her career to advocating for vulnerable children, particularly those affected by bullying in schools. Nancy's compassionate work extended beyond the counseling room as she authored several impactful books, offering guidance to parents on supporting their children through such challenges. In each publication, she tenderly dedicated her work to Tiffany, honoring her memory and perpetuating her legacy of compassion and resilience.

Stu's experience within the haunted mansion served as a catalyst for a significant academic shift. He successfully graduated from law school and now serves as a prosecuting attorney for a prominent county. Specializing in fraud investigations, particularly those targeting the elderly, Stu passionately pursues justice, safeguarding vulnerable communities from exploitation and deception.

Professor Daniel Sullivan's life took a divergent path following the haunting events and the heartbreaking loss of Tiffany. No longer delving into the realm of suspected spiritual charlatans, he now channels his expertise towards nurturing the minds of undergraduate students in the fundamentals of psychology. Content in his role, he imparts knowledge on Pavlov's famous experiments and Operant Conditioning, eschewing the complexities of parapsychology for more grounded subjects.

Despite his personal challenges, Daniel found creative solace in writing. His fictionalized account of the Zorba mansion's mysteries captured the imagination of many, eventually transforming into a screenplay that garnered significant attention, though it has yet to grace the silver screen. In his leisure time, Daniel embarks on contemplative drives to the former site of the Zorba estate, reflecting on the profound transformation that has transpired since those haunting days.

As he finds solace on a wooden bench nestled within the tranquility of Tiffany Park, his mind invariably wanders to the enigmatic fate of the original 13 ghosts. Recollections of that fateful night, haunted by the specter of Dr. Plato Zorba and the innocent souls he ensnared, linger in his thoughts. In his contemplation, he imagines the young victims, including Ann Zorba, finding peace in the embrace of the afterlife, while the sinister doctor and his killer, Benjamin Rush, face their deserved damnation in the depths of hell.

Yet, amidst these assumed destinies, questions persist. What became of the lion tamer and his majestic companion? Did the mad Italian chef and his terrified wife, alongside the other spectral inhabitants, find rest beyond the veil of mortality? As he gazes upon the serene expanse of the Francis Zorba community, he ponders whether echoes of the past still linger, concealed within the shadows of the verdant grounds.

These lingering uncertainties, shrouded in the mist of memory, weave themselves into the fabric of his consciousness, a testament to the enduring mysteries that dwell within the heart of Tiffany Park and the legacy of the Zorba estate. Though time may pass, these ponderings remain etched in his soul, a testament to the enduring allure of the unknown and the haunting specters of the past.

DIRECTOR AND CAST

William Castle
Director and Producer

Charles Herbert
"Buck"

Rosemary DeCamp
Hilda Zorba

Jo Morrow
Madea Zorba

Donald Woods
Cyrus Zorba

Martin Milner
Benjamin Rush

Margaret Hamilton
Elaine Zachariides

13
COLOR
GHOSTS
ILLUSION-O!

"Plenty of chills and chuckles." - LEONARD MALTIN
13
13 TIMES
THE THRILLS!
13 TIMES
THE SCREAMS!
13 TIMES
THE FUN!
GHOSTS
GHOST
STORIES
DVD
VIDEO

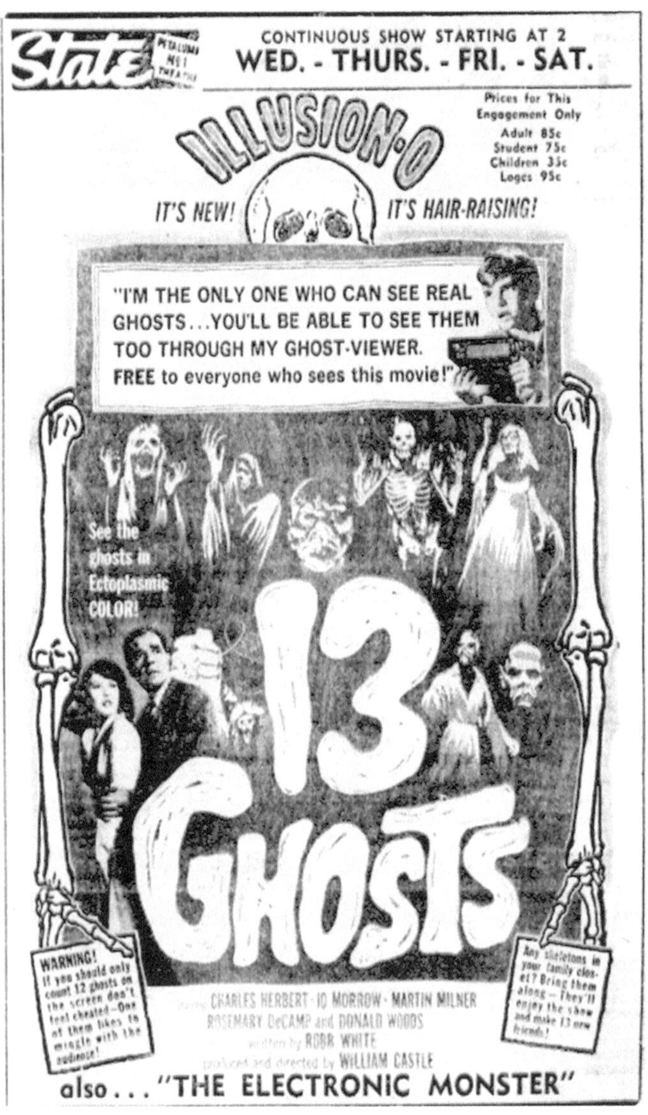
State
CONTINUOUS SHOW STARTING AT 2
WED. - THURS. - FRI. - SAT.
Prices for This Engagement Only
Adult 85c
Student 75c
Children 35c
Loges 95c
ILLUSION-O
IT'S NEW!
IT'S HAIR-RAISING!
"I'M THE ONLY ONE WHO CAN SEE REAL GHOSTS...YOU'LL BE ABLE TO SEE THEM TOO THROUGH MY GHOST-VIEWER. FREE to everyone who sees this movie!"
See the ghosts in Ectoplasmic COLOR!
13 GHOSTS
WARNING! If you should only count 12 ghosts on the screen don't feel cheated—One of them likes to mingle with the audience!
Any skeletons in your family closet? Bring them along — They'll enjoy the show and make 13 new friends!
CHARLES HERBERT · JO MORROW · MARTIN MILNER
ROSEMARY DeCAMP and DONALD WOODS
written by ROBB WHITE
produced and directed by WILLIAM CASTLE
also..."THE ELECTRONIC MONSTER"

13
COLOR
GHOSTS
ILLUSION-O!

13
COLOR
GHOSTS
ILLUSION-O!

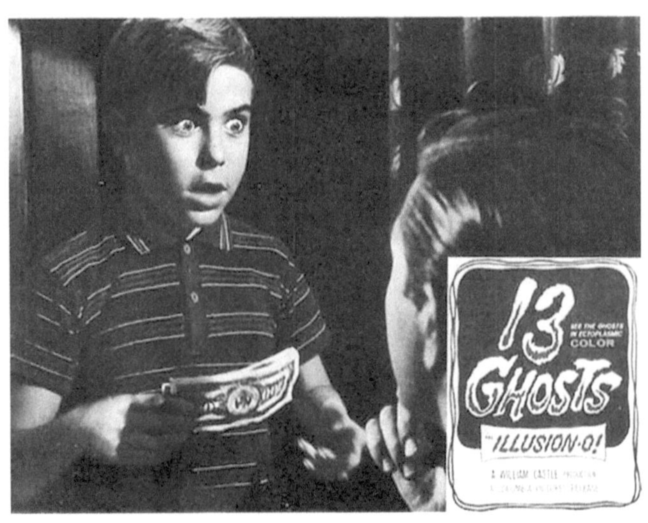
13
SEE THE GHOSTS IN ECTOPLASMIC COLOR
GHOSTS
ILLUSION-O!
A WILLIAM CASTLE PRODUCTION

SHADRACK
THE GREAT
13
SEE THE GHOSTS IN ECTOPLASMIC COLOR
GHOSTS
ILLUSION-O!
A WILLIAM CASTLE PRODUCTION

www.ingramcontent.com/pod-product-compliance
Lightning Source LLC
Chambersburg PA
CBHW020558310726
48979CB00008B/1262/J

* 9 7 9 8 9 9 0 7 2 5 4 0 9 *